RED WORLD

Book One

Jamie Lynn

CHAPTER ONE

Sean

You coming to the after party at Dave and Manik's?" My best friend Scotty yelled at me from across the crowded bar.

I shook my head and pointed to my watch, "I have to get up early to catch my flight! Tell them congratulations on the big win!"

"Where is your next shoot?" Scotty yelled.

"England! Bucket list, *CHECK*!" I yelled, making the check mark sign in the air.

Scotty had the decency to at least attempt to hide the jealousy. I knew he wanted to go on this assignment too, but the director wanted to go a different route apparently. Scotty was tall, muscular and drop-dead gorgeous. He had a tendency to be a bit too bossy for a bottom though. I had never worked with him before directly, but I was told from guys that had that Scotty

3

just couldn't seem to lose the top-tude. He was a switch, same as me, but I think he just needed to stick to being a top. Me on the other hand, I liked both. Which was why I had gotten the gig. I knew I wasn't as handsome as Scotty. Nor did my five-five compare to his six-two. I also wasn't as muscular, and I had a few regrettable tattoos, and there was that annoying scar on my lip from fixing my cleft lip as a baby.

I didn't get booked as often as the *'big names'* in our company, but requests for me on assignments were starting to pick up. This one would last two weeks, all expenses paid and I would be doing a grueling eight shoots. Thankfully, three of them were pretty tame stuff. Including a *'first time'* themed one. That was going to be pretty funny. I had to act all innocent and nervous. The scripts were decent, or at least not downright stupid and the pay... omg. The pay was enough that I was going to be able to finally have enough for the down payment on a house. I was twenty-three and the thought of owning my own home... God, it was practically a turn on in and of itself.

I climbed into one of the cabs that were wisely lined up along the street in front of the bar and gave him my address.

"You at that party in there?"

"Yeah, it was wild!"

"Was it really a porn awards show?"

"Yes, indeed it was. Two of my friends got awards, and our company got a special award for having the highest approval rating of any of the companies whose employees were polled."

"Wow. So it's like... awards for the best tits in a water scene?"

"Ahhh, no. Sorry. However, the winners will be posted on the awards show website." I told him with a grin.

"So, you do any big name chicks?" The guy grinned toothily.

I quirked an eyebrow, "Actually yes. I had a threesome scene with Jasmin Jets."

The car swerved a bit, "Sorry... are you serious?"

"Yep. She's a total sweetheart. She brought us cupcakes before the shoot."

"What was she like? Are her tits real? My brother says they are fake."

"Sadly... like most of the women in the business, yes. They are fake." I laughed, "But she went to the best surgeon around and frankly, he does amazing work."

"No joke! I could fuck those titties for weeks!" I began to suspect the guy was jacking off when the car swerved again, and he had only one hand on the wheel. Just great!

"Yeah, they are nice and so is she, she's a really nice person." I felt the need to stand up Jasmine, who had become one of my best friends.

"Yeah, yeah... sure she is. Does she fake orgasm or is she really squeezing like a vise?" The car swerved again.

"Either get your hand off your cock and back on the wheel or pull over and let me out. I don't want to die today, just so you can jack off." I raised my eyebrow at him.

He suddenly swerved to the side of the road, "So, does she really squirt like that or is that a staged thing?"

I grabbed just enough to cover what the meter said and threw the money at him. I got out and started to walk. Sure enough... he was rapidly jerking as he drove. Good God. Have some self-control, man!

"You know... I'm not sure, I was too busy fucking the guy that was fucking her to notice. He was really hot! Total apple butt and a noisy little thing too! It was his first shoot... his first time, too. You might like to look that one up!"

"You're a faggot?!" The guy looked like he was going to swerve into me, "I'm Bi and a switch. I'm versatile like that. Makes for a more interesting scene. Guy on girl gets so boring."

The guy drove away with tires screeching. He swerved the taxi into the oncoming lane, and nearly had a head-on collision with another car. I had wondered if bursting his bubble would be a turn-off, apparently not... not that he would admit it. Who watches porn with their brother anyway?! Ewww!

I looked around and grumbled. At least I wasn't terribly far from home. I knew the area fairly well, and this neighborhood was only about a mile from my house. Granted, walking down the side of this particular road at three AM would probably get me propositioned or at the very least have people offer. I hated my neighborhood, but when I got my place it was all that my twenty-one year-old college dropout ass could afford.

I had only gone about a quarter mile when I felt something sting me in the back. I jumped and tried to turn around only to find the ground rapidly rising up to meet me. My forehead kissed pavement and my eyes blurred with the force of the impact.

For a moment, I wondered if Jerk-off-Joe the Cabbie had come back and shot me. I realized then that other than the intense pounding in my head from where I had hit the pavement, my back didn't hurt like I would expect being shot would cause. I also couldn't move a damned thing. I could hardly even move my eyes. Was that from the blow to the head? I was starting to panic when I felt myself being rolled over.

Four identical and extremely large men looked down at me. They didn't just look alike. They were identical. As in completely fucking identical. One of them nodded to another, who leaned down and picked me up as easily as if I were made of rags and not flesh, bone, and muscle. Not to mention blood was rapidly flowing from my forehead and cheek from where I had kissed the pavement. I could feel my eye already swelling. I felt the brute suddenly swung me off his shoulder and flop me into the back of what looked like a moving van.

Well, except for the multiple levels of cages where men and women were piled neatly on top of each other. I was slid into a cage on the bottom row, and I landed on my back with my head dropping painfully onto the floor. The guy didn't apologize, he just reached up and lowered the door and pressed it into the cage until it made a whirring sound and a click.

Oh my fucking God. I've been kidnapped by human traffickers! This wasn't good! I tried to get my body to move. I blinked my eyes harder and harder. That backfired quickly because it only served to get more of my sticky blood to flow into my eyes. I had to close them to keep the blood out. Then, I realized in horror, my eyelids stayed down. I tried over and over to open them, but nothing worked other than my hearing.

The door opened and closed at least a dozen, maybe even two dozen times. A lightweight body was dropped onto my chest. I was guessing that was a female by the size and strong scent of perfume. After the cage door was closed again, I felt the truck roar to life. It began to bob and sway as we turned out onto the main road. I felt them go past the intersection that I always took to get to my apartment with its rattling man-hole cover.

I realized with horror that because I was scheduled to fly out in the morning, it was likely no one would figure out that I was missing until I didn't show for the shoot which wouldn't be until two days after I was meant to arrive. I was so fucked!! I tried to move again and not even a hint of movement happened anywhere in my body except the rise and fall of my chest, which, although a bit faster than normal was regular and seemed unaffected by whatever medicine caused this total body paralysis.

We were driven for about twenty minutes before I felt us turn right at an intersection and we took a hard bounce that banged my head into the cage floor with a meaty think. I was not the only one who would likely have a concussion after this ride. The moving truck slowed and came to a stop. I could hear the doors open and the sound of someone climbing in. I heard a conversation in a language that I was completely unfamiliar with.

I felt a jolt of movement, and the cage was suddenly being pulled out of the position it was in, and we were rolled down the moving van's ramp and across a room that echoed hollowly. It was cold, damp, and smelled of rot. I could also smell that oh-so-attractive low tide smell that can only happen at the dockyards. This place had to be one of the abandoned warehouses past the marina.

I felt the cage being lifted and we were slid into something that seemed much smaller. The sounds disappeared as we were suddenly being lifted and slid forward at an angle upward for quite a distance before we were spun roughly to the side then moved forward a short distance. I heard a hollow clank, and a thump that was reminiscent of my refrigerator door closing. There was a hissing sound that I knew instantly was the sound of a gas being pumped into the cage.

I tried to force my eyes open as the gas took hold of my mind. The cage began to feel bitterly cold and more and more gas poured in. Suddenly, I heard the sound of water. My mind was now frantic. I could feel my mind trying to rationalize my way out of this, to come up with a plan. There was no plan! I was royally fucked! I felt water slowly come up over my side. I felt the woman who was on top of me slip slightly and I knew she was now underwater.

She was drowning leaning against my chest and I could do nothing suddenly the water was up to my still bleeding cheek. It was so cold that it burned! My body was screaming in pain. If I could have shaken myself apart limb from limb I would have but my body didn't so much as quiver. I felt it move over my eye and then to the side of my mouth and nose. In seconds it flooded over my nose and mouth. I tried to hold my breath, but I was shocked when my body kept breathing against my will. The water began to flood into my mouth, up my nose, down my throat. I felt the icy water rapidly fill my lungs.

Seconds passed and the water was now over my head. I felt the last bubbles of air escaping from my body as I began to lift up with the raising of the water. My lungs slowed and then I felt them stop. I couldn't breathe. I felt my heart start to stutter. It missed beats, then it too began to slow.

Suddenly my eyes began to open as the blood that had dried onto my lashes came loose in the water. I saw a solid ceiling above my head, just above the mesh that my body now rested against. I felt my heart spasm frantically. I was about to die!

My last conscious thought before the darkness overcame my mind was that I really should have gone to Dave and Manik's after party.

CHAPTER TWO

De'Ceer

Are you done yet?" My little brother whined and slowly shambled down the nearly deserted outdoor market place. He kicked at the dry red sand, which of course sent it flying right into my face.

"Relin! Need I remind you, you are the one who begged to come today? You whined at father that you never get to spend time with me anymore. I told you I had to work today. I told you it would be boring for you."

"But... you're a market security enforcer! Why aren't you stopping thieves, catching swindlers, doing anything! Today I've seen you drink four cups of lein tea, eat five rodash skewers, flirt with at least two dozen females... females who by the way were only teasing you. And the best thing?! You took a two light mark long nap on that sunning rock! Is this what you do all day?"

I paused before shrugging, "Some days are a bit slower

than others. Today is mid lunar cycle. That's always a slow day unless it has a festival of events on it. Today is when most of the females come out with their guards to do their shopping. And yes, I know they were only flirting. None of them would select me and I am alright with that. Most of them were betrothed before they shed their hatchling scales."

"And the two light cycle nap?"

"I have a one light cycle break for feeding... I... overslept a bit. That is why I am staying an extra hour to make sure I log the correct number of hours."

"Oh, elder brother... did you really fight for the right to be an enforcer just to flirt with unavailable females and take naps in the sun?"

I spun around and glared at my brother, "No, I fought for the right so that you and others of our cast will have the right to become enforcers. I am not unaware that I have been given a shit job... but it's a *JOB*."

"You would have earned more credits working with father in the mine."

"Possibly." I sighed. "Probably. That's not the point. The point is that I fought for this job so that others of our caste can be more than dirt diggers."

"I don't think they want to if this is all they will get." My brother scowled at me.

"This isn't ideal, but this is how change starts. By one

person being willing to take a chance and to stand up for something," I looked at him. My younger brother was exactly like our father. Our father spent all day, nine days a cycle digging in the mines just to have one day off before doing it all over again. He started doing it when he was younger than Relin and he will likely die doing it of the black cough long before old age should take him from us. I wanted more for my little brother and it scared me that Relin couldn't see that there was more to life than scratching in the dirt to look for shiny things that the wealthy mine owners take and sell off world for what I am sure are sizable fortunes. My father, meanwhile, still has another eight years before he pays off his purchase debt to the mine. Then, he will be free to go, with nothing in his pocket and black dust suffocating the life out of him.

Our mother was an off world female. She had come here with the slave auction and had failed to sell because she had only one eye and a scar that crossed her lips from a knife wound. She was left to die of dehydration or predator attack after the auction ended. My father found her, nearly dead from dehydration. He took her home, gave her his own water supply for two days and drank the putrid water in the mine to stay alive.

Our mother survived and ultimately proved to be compatible with my father and they produced four offspring. The first two were taken by the mine owner. We do not know what happened to them. Then I was born missing my digging claws and I was left to my parents to raise. My younger brother was born years later and has only minimal digging claws. He does not understand that he will likely never be allowed to mine. It would be a waste of time if he could not cleave the hard soil apart with his short and stubby claws. I knew that he must have realized it by now, but he still hung on to the hope that he could work alongside our father.

I turned and walked toward the stone hut that served as the market enforcement office. I retrieved my time card and used a small sharp tool I carry in my tool belt to punch my card to sign out. I slid it into the pay box and waved my brother out the door. In a matter of a few short minutes, the weather had begun to shift dramatically. The air, which had been still and quiet all day began to blow in brief guts bringing with it the first of the fine dust that indicated an approaching sand storm.

I grabbed my brother and hurried along through the market. The venders frantically stowed their wares and sealed their stall hatches closed. They hurried past us in the other direction, away from the storm. They could use any of the three merchant caste shelters located in convenient locations around the market. Likewise, the few shoppers still left could go to the public shelters, there were six within a few minutes run from the market just in case a storm were to hit on a crowded shopping day or on a festival.

My brother and I could use none of them. Neither could we use the warrior's shelters. Even though I was an enforcer and therefore, technically, considered to be a warrior no one of my caste was ever allowed inside. The only way in was if someone from a higher caste, such as a warrior, personally brought us inside and as far as I knew, it had never happened. My brother and I ran as fast as we could, closing our eyes and nostrils to the tightest slits possible to keep the sand out. My brother was losing ground and slowing. He was not strong enough to fight the wind and his short toe claws could not get purchase on the shifting sand or the under rock. I grabbed him and pulled him to the side of the nearest building. I wrapped him in my arms and carried him through the blinding sand. We were close to the shelter when I tripped over something which was lying under a mound of sand.

I reached down, and to my horror, felt an arm. Without thinking, I grabbed the body and picked it up, throwing it up into my chest, over my brother and continuing to fight the last distance to the only shelter available to us. The slave shelters were always massively overcrowded during a storm. They seldom had any supplies and on the rare case they did, they were typically rancid. I passed through the multiple layers of heavy cloth that did little to keep the sand out and ran as quickly as I dared away from the rapidly increasing storm. I could feel the static charge beginning. This would be one heck of a lightning storm, probably the worse in a year or two, hopefully not more.

I reached the end of the blowout tunnel and kicked at the door. It was opened and I shoved my way through. I looked around at the dimly lit room. People stood, or if they were lucky, sat, shoulder to shoulder or any many cases, one on top of each other. The weight in my arms was growing harder to manage by the second. I finally spotted an empty place up on the top tier on the far side of the room. Not a good place. Hundreds of storms had worn away this side of the building to the point that there were now gaps in the thick stone where the mortar had been worn away.

I carried them up to the top tier and settled down on the pile of sand which had already blown in over the past storms. I took off my over cloak and draped it over the three of us. I examined my brother, he was terrified to put it mildly. Having spent most of his life in the burrows where he would be safe from the ravages of the desert planets wrath, he had little experience with the harsher truths about this world. It was heartless. It could kill or maim in an instant or it could drag death out for years.

My brother curled into a little ball with his tail wrapped tightly over his nose. I had not seen him take a hatchling pose in over five years since he had climbed from our mother's nest for the first time. Always so brave and sure of himself, now he looked like a terrified child and I wished again that I had not brought him with me today. I hoped that it would not leave him traumatized. Though he thought himself big and strong, he was still only seven cycles. He would not reach maturity for another fifteen.

I looked to the body that I had picked up along the way. It was an off worlder, the sand was caked to its body. It appeared to be coated in mud. Mud? The mixture of sand and water? Why would an outsider be covered in something so precious? I carefully scrapped the clumps of mud away from his eyes, blessedly, they were sealed shut with long lashes that had likely kept the sand out. His nostrils, however, were wide open and mud was caked up inside of them. I reached for my card punching tool and used it to scrap his nostrils free. His skin was so soft. I was shocked by his lack of scales. He was as soft as a newborn hatchling. I shook with shock. Was he a newly hatched? I looked down at his strange garments and quickly dismissed that idea.

I looked at his hands, they had four fingers had three

segments and ended in dull slick claws that never had any hope of cutting anything at all. I brushed his long matted hair back and was startled to see the protruding shapes of flesh on the sides of his head. He had a matching one on the other side. I used my dull fingers to clean them out until I suddenly found his ears. That strange shaped flesh must form a cone around his ear holes to make them more effective, but clearly they were not an advantage in a sandstorm as they channeled the sand down into his ear holes which did not appear to be able to close.

The strangers breathing was rough, he coughed frequently, but had not been able to move. I had an idea, I turned him over and draped him across my lap and slid my hand down his back feeling for markers. He had a spine, but I felt no spinal ridge to protect. I brushed his hair away and was shocked to see that his neck had no protection at all. I felt his rib cage and determined the location of his breathing lungs. I began to sharply slap him on the back with the flat of my palm.

A few strong slaps and he gagged and a mind boggling amount of water came up from his chest. I hit his back again and again until his breathing sounded clear. Seeing water flood out of a person's mouth had gotten us quite a lot of unwanted attention. Many people glared at the puddle on the ground in disgust. Water was never to be wasted. Even our bodily fluids were collected to be purified.

I ran my hand over his head and suddenly felt a large lump on the back of his head. It did not feel natural as it was swollen and off center. I turned him over and held up and looked closer at his face. I could now make out blood slowly seeping through a large gash on his forehead and another across his cheek. I used my hand to wipe more sand away from his face. I saw a fairly noticeable scar that ran from the inside of his nostril down to his lip. His lip pulled up slightly to the side. I had not noticed it at first, but it reminded me of my mother's scar.

Then it dawned on me. My mother had once told me that when she was captured from her world she and others of her kind and been locked in a cage and submerged in a water. She had been unable to move until her lungs succumbed to the water and her heart stopped. She awoke as she was dumped out onto the auction platform. When her scars and missing eye were noticed she was branded as defective and had been cruelly drug out of the auction house by her foot and left outside of the gates. The auction house was within a few minutes' walk down the same path we had been coming up to seek shelter.

I began to search him for a defective mark. I pulled up the arm sections of his garment, I pulled up the leg sections, I then lifted the torso covering and there I found it. The skin angry and blistered, still bleeding though mostly cauterized. The mark that meant he had not been sold and would be left to die or to be claimed by whatever person happened upon him. I looked over his fine features, they were beautiful, in a strange sort of way. His hair as it dried looked less dark and almost looked like the golden hues of the sky after a sandstorm passes and the electrical charge has dissipated.

I remembered my mother saying she lay unable to move for two cycles where she had been dropped. She had been poked over, and even abused by males who then left her to lie there and die.

This male had either been carried all this way or had somehow managed to walk away from the storm. I tested his reflexes by pinching the thin web of skin between his short thumb and his finger. His finger gave the tiniest twitch. No. He had not walked on his own. Someone had tried to claim him only to be overtaken by the storm. Considering that they had passed the slave shelter it would have to be a higher caste person, but why? Did they want a new toy to play with?

I felt a growl build in my throat at the thought. I pulled the male into a sitting position and pulled him back against my chest. I leaned his head back on my shoulder and wrapped my arms around him. I began to run my hands down my brother's spinal scales to try to calm him as the storm worsened. I pulled him closer until I was able to lift him to place him in the off worlder's lap. His body had warmed significantly since I had first picked him up. I dropped my cloak over the three of us to protect us from the fine dust that was now blowing through the crack over our head. The male coughed frequently and more water would come up from time to time. I felt his head begin to twitch until it finally rolled against my neck.

It was an alarmingly sexual position. The small gaps between the hard scales on the sides of our neck were highly sensitive and his breath was shockingly hot. It felt like he was radiating heat from within. We could not produce our own heat and therefor had to either bask under the sun to gain enough heat to go to our burrows at night or we had to use the public warming stones in the burrows. They were frequently filthy and I cringed to think that my father and brother used them daily. My mother only needed them seasonally when the temperature dropped in the burrows.

If the sandstorm lasted too long, people would begin to drop into cold shock. The other shelters had supplies to help them cope with the cold, but here in the slave shelters, the longer that the storm raged, the more people were going to die.

I turned to look at the stranger in my arms. Holding him was like holding a living heating stone. I could feel my body responding in ways I had never felt before. I shifted uncomfortably as I felt my shaft attempt to breach my cloaca. I attempted to tighten my abdominal muscles, trying to stop my shaft from swelling. The feeling of the male's body heat pressing against my lap was an exquisite torture. I slid my hands tighter around his torso. The heat he was giving off warmed my entire body as the temperature outside began to drop steadily.

Fearing that my brother would become too cold, I shifted him off the male's lap and turned us onto our sides. I pulled his knees up into as close of an approximation of a hatchling position as I thought he could comfortably make before carefully placing my brother against the strangers stomach and legs. I pulled his arms around my brother and then coiled my body protectively around both of them. I shook my cloak off, and received several snarls from nearby people, before draping my cloak around us. I left breathing room around the edges, but I made sure that the hard leather of my cloak was between us and the now fridge stones.

I could hear the static cracking before the bolts of the enormous storm were unleashed in close proximity to our shelter. Many people screamed in panic. I felt the male in my arms tense. He may not be able to move, but I had a feeling he was at least somewhat aware of what was happening around him. Keeping that in mind, I schooled my body to stop reacting to his heat. I felt him cough and this time he made a low moan. He panted and moaned again. I wondered if his neck was hurting as his head looked to be at an uncomfortable angle, tipped downward to the ground. I slid my arm under his head and rested the side of my face on his amazingly soft neck. His body heat felt so good that without meaning to, I began rub the scent glands under my chin onto his neck and shoulder. I pulled him closer, scenting myself on him. It felt so incredible and completely right. I felt like I was exactly where I was meant to be.

CHAPTER THREE

Sean

I woke with a start as my body was dumped unceremoniously out of the cage and onto a rough grate. I felt a tube being shoved down my throat and a large amount of water being pumped out as air was being pushed back in. I felt my lungs beginning to work again as my blood began its horrific march through my veins. I felt like every cell was being burned alive. I felt my arms slowly softening and dropping to lay by my sides. I realized that while my brain had apparently been thawed out, the rest of me was still a bit frozen.

I had been frozen. Like a human Popsicle. I knew, or at least believed that humans do not have the technology to freeze and reanimate a human body. That left me to ponder two possibilities. Number one: some underground ring of human traffickers had invented a technology that could make them insanely rich, but were using it to smuggle people. Or number two: those identical strange looking men who shot me in the back were aliens.

As much as it pained me to think about it, the simple fact is that it was more likely that I had just been kidnaped by aliens. My eyes were closed, but I could make out light from dark through my closed lids. Whatever surface I lay upon was uncomfortable, but also extremely hot. My body burned more and more as it thawed.

Just as I began to cough to bring up more water I felt the table I had been lying on tilt suddenly to the side. I felt my body sliding painfully over the rough surface before skidding to a stop on something that felt dry and gritty. I heard loud sounds and shouting. Then someone was digging through my clothing, looking everywhere, even down my pants. When the rough hands with sharp points came to my face, it gripped my head and turned it back and forth. My eyes were forced open and I saw for the first time who had been man handling me.

It was a creature that looked essentially reptilian with scaly skin and a mostly smooth rounded head, except for the unruly hair that hung down over the sides of its head in thick cords. Its eyes were golden in hue and slit vertically. I felt it focus on my mouth. My lip and nose were examined as well as my teeth. There were loud shouts and then silence. I felt my shirt being lifted and suddenly there was a searing pain in the center of my chest. I felt something that could only be a brand being pushed deep into my skin and rocked back and forth before it was ripped away. I could smell the stench of my own burning flesh and the agony was so intense that I believed I was going to die.... Again. I felt something grab my leg and I was given a hard yank. I crashed to the ground several feet below, once again striking the back of my already throbbing head. I felt myself being drug along. Little to no care was given to ensure I was not slammed into objects or at one point, stepped on.

I was finally thrown out into what could only be a busy street. I could hear the sounds of people talking, smell food being cooked, what I suspected was animals sniffing about, and the ever present sound of the room I had just left. It did not take long to realize that it was an auction. I had just been run through an auction and now I lay on the side of a street. I suspected they had not been pleased with my scar.

Was that a good thing or was it bad?

I felt myself being poked and prodded on occasion, but none stayed long. I felt what could only be a hot sun beating down upon me. I felt my skin being burned by the heat at the same time I was thawing out. I felt something grab my arm and begin to drag me along again. I was pulled for what had to be several blocks before I heard a powerful sounding voice booming over me. Then a smaller voice whining before I felt the hand being ripped away from my hand. I heard it crying as the sounds grew more distant. I suspected that was the alien equivalent of *'look at this lost puppy I found on the way home, can I keep it'?*

As I lay in a crumpled heap on a mound of sand until I began to feel a strange movement in the air. A wind was picking up and with it came a super fine dust and the electric scent of an approaching storm. I knew this was likely a bad thing. I kept trying to fight the paralysis until I felt something very large and heavy trip and fall on top of me. I felt myself being heaved up into the air and into the full force of the wind as I was thrown over someone's shoulder like a sack of potatoes. . I felt whoever was carrying me struggle to keep his footing. I could feel another body underneath mine. I tried to open my eyes, but all I could make out was something switching back and it looked to be coming from the guys' ass.... Omg. This guy has a *TAIL*!

I was forced to pinch my eyes closed to keep the sand out as it swirled around us. I breathed as carefully as I could through pinched lips. Thankfully, my face was now pressing into the creatures back and while my nose was hopelessly clogged with sand the upside down position did help to clear more water from my lungs. My breathing became less labored even with the sand.

I felt the creature shoving its way between many layers of some sort of heavy rough cloth and then down a long space where I could hear sounds echoing off nearby walls. The wind was non-existant here at least. I felt and heard him come to a stop and kick at a door which slowly groaned open before clanking shut again.

The creature paused for a moment in the dark room before turning to carry us up a long flight of stairs. He finally came to a stop and lowered us to the ground. I felt him move me over to get to the smaller shape, it was a few seconds before I felt his hands on my skin. He was brushing sand away from my eyes, my mouth and then using something slender and downright scary to clean out my nose. I felt him touch my ears before cleaning them out as well. Not long after that I felt him examine me all over. At least he had not opened my pants to look down them.

As rough as the previous aliens had been, this one was gentle. I felt his smooth, cool fingers trace over my face before I was roughly turned over to a face down position across his lap. The only time I had been in this position was when my dad was about to spank me. I felt him feel around my head, neck, ribs, and spine before giving me several hard pats on my back. I felt the water finally escaping my lungs. I was able to cough more deeply and that brought up more water. He was not satisfied until I stopped panting for air.

I felt him grab me and turn me to sit on the ground in front of me before he carefully lifts me up and then settles me on his lap. I felt him place something against my lap before fabric being thrown over our heads. Eventually, I began to notice the tightening of the creature's arms around me, I felt his body shift under me and I realized he was probably aroused, because of the swelling I was feeling against my backside.

Strangely, it turned me on a bit to know that I was held tight in his arms.

As the storm continued to rage, I felt him lift the smaller balled up creature off my lap before be turned me onto my side and slid me into the fetal position. He replaced the creature against my middle and I braced for whatever was to come. I felt it pull tight around me, draping its tail around my body and using the tip to caress my head. Its hands explored my body slowly, almost subconsciously. I felt my body heat finally rise and with it, so did his inability to sit still. He squirmed constantly, shifting his hips against my ass and then pulling it away. I wondered if he was waiting for me to make the same move. I kept trying to move until finally I was able to tip my head to the side. I felt my body respond with a low moan to his presence.

I felt his hands around me tighten before he covered us with the cloth. I felt as he slowly pushed his face into my neck and began to rub his chin over my flesh. It felt rough and odd, but not painful. Nothing with him had been painful... yet. I realized that the slight musky scent that I had been smelling since my nose was more or less clean now was getting stronger. I liked the scent, it was both calming and relaxing.

His body was so cool to the touch that I began to suspect that he was actually cold blooded. The warmer I got, the more he pressed into my body. I probably felt great to him, but I felt chilled wherever his body touched.

As the time passed slowly the roaring of the wind increased. The lightning became so ferocious that it seemed like one constant crackle. I tried to relax into his body, but my limbs were beginning to jump and twitch. I was getting very uncomfortable. I felt like I needed to move my limbs to shake them awake. As the twitches and jerks became more noticeable I felt his hand slide to wherever was twitching. He seemed to be trying to calm me or comfort me.

I finally felt my vocal cords start to stir to life when I was able to make a tiny moan. He lay his head against mine and rubbed the side of his rough cheek against my smooth one. The fact that I still didn't have much stubble was not terribly surprising. I never grew much facial hair to begin with. When I did, I looked like that guy in high school that tries to grow a mustache to look older and ends up looking creepy instead. So, in lieu of carrying around a razor with me all of the time I went for a more permanent solution. I also had permanent hair removal on my chest and back. I let my legs and groin be a bit hairy.

My mind wandered as time slowly passed. I thought about everything I would miss back home. I thought about the house I would never be able to buy. I thought about the husband and children that I would never be able to have. Yes, I'm a gay man... well... bi man... but I always had a strong desire to have children. Not necessarily children that I 'sired' so to speak, but it was a dream since I was in high school.

I twitched strongly and my hips jerked backwards, slamming my ass into his groin. I heard him grunt at the impact. He pulled back for a moment and I managed to whimper.

I heard him make low murmuring sounds as he ran his hand down my side. He moved closer again and I felt something very large, and very hard pressing against my ass. Well! Looks like someone likes being pressed up against his own personal heating buddy.

I felt the small thing that I was curled around me begin to unfurl. I felt a smaller body wriggle closer to mine. I heard a quiet purring sound begin and felt a smaller head shove its way in against my neck. I realized this was likely a small child. They pushed in close to my body and I felt a small arm wrap around my torso just before the one behind me wrapped his arm over mine to touch the small one. I was between their bodies and despite the fact that I had no idea who they were, I felt safe.

Their breathing evened out as the storm raged on outside. When I was finally able to move my limbs again, I turned slightly to relieve the pressure on my shoulder. I realized with a start that my eyes were finally starting to open. I looked around the very dimly lit space under the heavy blanket. The air we were not breathing was hot, humid, and smelled shockingly strong of the musk. I was beginning to really like that smell. I wanted more of it.

I pushed back into him while turning my head. I wasn't able to get a glimpse of him, but I could see the top of the smaller one's head. They had tangled rust colored hair that was thicker than human hair. I realized he must be the same species as the one I remembered from when I was first awoken. I was not happy to know that I was not cuddled between two of them, but these two at least had not harmed me. I tried to reserve judgment until I had more information.

With great effort, I was able to raise my hand and flick more sand away. I then carefully wiped the sand out of my eyes and began to blow my nose. Ok, it was gross. I will admit it. But it was necessary to blow more than a few snot rockets before my nose was finally clear enough that I could breathe easier.

The one behind me stirred, but settled back to sleep again. I realized that the ground beneath us was now terribly cold. We had nothing under us and I could feel the little one trying to get away from the cold and closer to me. I slid my arm under him and rolled to my back. Holding him on my chest would keep him warmer at least. He stretched out and made another purring sound contentedly as I lay my own head back on the arm of the other male. Sometime later I finally dozed off into a deep dreamless sleep.

CHAPTER FOUR

De'Ceer

I woke to the sound of the storm watcher at the door banging the storm clear alert. I blinked before I realized why I was so sluggish. I curled closer to the warm male. My mind slowly began to process again and I sat up slowly and painfully. I carefully slid back and left my cloak draped over them. I realized the temperature in the room was fringed. I felt it begin to chill me immediately. I looked around. Not a single person around me was moving. Hundreds of bodies lay stretched or coiled throughout the room. Warriors were dragging the bodies outside to lay them in the sun. If they had any hope of survival it was to get them warmed as quickly as possible

I carefully lifted my cloak up and let the sand slide off slowly. I looked down into the single most beautiful pair of eyes I had ever seen. The eyes were white with a circle of a color I had never even seen before. They sparkled with threads of brighter colors. The centers were like tiny pools of black. The long lashes formed a frame around the eyes that made me shudder with his beauty.

I suddenly shook out of my shock and looked down for my brother. I found him draped across the off worlder's chest. He had put my brother on his chest to protect him from the cold. It hit me hard that he had just saved my brother's life. It was unlikely that he would have survived this cold without the extra heat the offworlder provided. I owed him a life debt. I leaned down and pressed our foreheads together in a sign of respect and bonding. It was something that was reserved for a treasured few in a person's life.

I pulled back and began to examine my brother. He stirred and chirped in distress. Even with the extra heat he was suffering from cold shock. I had to get him outside quickly. I lifted him to my chest before letting the off worlder try to stand. He was shaky and clearly very weak. I reached my arm around him and under his opposite arm. I grabbed my cloak and threw it over my front and my shoulder. I did not want my brother to remember laying in a room with hundreds of dead bodies.

We slowly made our way through the sea of bodies to where the storm watcher stood. His scales were pale with shock.

"Enforcer? You live? Here I thought all here were dead."

"I and my brother and an off worlder who is in my charge survived. Are there any others showing signs of recovery?

His head fell before it shook slightly. The magnitude of the disaster on the slaves in our shelter struck me. I also realized that my parents now likely thought they had lost both their sons. I hurried to get us outside. I saw a sea of bodies already laid out on the heaping mounds of sand that had filled the streets. The sound of people wailing in grief filled the air. As bodies were identified, they were carried to the recycling center by their loved ones. Nothing was wasted in this world of such precious few resources.

I walked toward our home area while the heat of the sun began to chase away the last of the chill. My brother began to stir against my chest.

"Lay still brother. I am taking us home. The storm is over. We both live another day." My brother purred and lay his head back on my shoulder again.

I had to pause for rest several times. I realized that it was nearly cruel to make the off worlder walk through the deep sand when he was only just over the paralysis. People raced past us toward the slave shelter as word of the tragedy spread. I was nearly home when I spotted my parents running as fast as they could across the sand. As soon as they spotted me, I heard my mother bellow in relief. She ran to me and I let her pull the cloak off of my brother. She grabbed him off my chest and pulled him into her arms as she collapsed in emotional wailing.

My father wrapped his arms around me tightly and for the first time in my life, I saw my father cry. He pressed out foreheads together and he held the sides of my face in his rough, scarred hands. When he pulled back, he looked at the off worlder with curiosity.

"I will explain at home. Please, can we go home?" My own emotion started to overcome me. I felt the off worlder reach his arm around me. He leaned his head on my shoulder for comfort. I turned, heedless of who watched and pressed our foreheads together. I wrapped my arms around him and held him tight. When we parted my father must have guessed that the reason he had his sons was because of the stranger before him.

He reached of the off worlder and pulled him close for a forehead press as well. In doing so he felt the heat coming off the off worlders skin. He turned to look at me and I nodded. We were alive because this unknown species produces its own heat from within. He nodded at me slightly before helping my mother to her feet. I tried not to look at the anguished and angry faces around us from people who had lost their loved ones. I knew there were many who would question how we survived. Bad rumors would spread, but my concern was for the off worlder's safety. In all our universe, no species produced its own life heat. He must have come from very far away indeed.

My father opened the door to our house and led us inside. My father guided the off worlder to sit in his own chair. He went and got him some of our water supply. He drank it quickly before making the most beautiful sounds I had ever heard. His voice was light, smooth and sounded more like music than language. My father inclined his head at what he took as a being thanked.

My mother held my little brother and rocked him as she had when he was a hatchling. He clung to her and wrapped his tail around her arm, refusing to let go. I went to him and leaned down to rub my chin over his head. My mother reached up and pressed our foreheads together.

"He saved you and Relin, didn't he."

"Yes, mother. He is an off worlder who was brought here as you were. Like you, he was marked and abandoned. I found him under a mound of blowing sand as I fought to carry Relin to the shelter. I got us inside, I believe we were likely the last to make it to the shelter."

"The storm was massive. They are trying to dig out the public heating stone as quickly as possible. People are even taking their eggs and hatchlings up onto the sands."

I nodded. I knew it would be bad here as well, but my mother had no idea of the scope of the disaster, "Mother, he saved our lives. The shelter became a frigid death trap. As far as I know he, Relin and I were the only ones out of hundreds, maybe a thousand to survive."

My mother's mouth slowly opened. Her hand went to her mouth in shock, "They are all dead?"

I closed my eyes, "The storm watch believes so. They are pulling the bodies out onto the sand to see if any survive and so they can be identified by their families."

My mother clutched Relin to her chest and began to cry. My mother would have been in the city working if it had not been her day of rest. If she had been in the city, she would have been at another slave shelter on the other side of town, and it was usually in worse condition than the one we had used. If all of the slave shelters failed, the death toll would be counted in the tens of thousands.

I let my father take my place comforting my mother and I returned to the off worlder. I reached my hand out to him and pulled him to his feet. I owed him a life debt, but moreover, I felt a strong connection to this male. I took him to my sleeping quarters and took him inside. I left him sitting on my fur pallet while I retrieved a pan of water and several washing rags. I also grabbed my mother's injury kit.

When I went back in the room, I saw him running his hands along the soft furs of my bed. I killed every one of them myself. My mother taught me how to turn them into beautiful hides. Her people were more knowledgeable about these things than mine.

I set the bowl and kit down before laying the rags at his feet. I tugged at his shirt and he reached down to grab the bottom of it before pulling it over his head. His body was so much different from my own. He had no protective scales anywhere. In fact, I found not a single scale at all. He had two strange round disks of color on each side of his chest. Each had a small nub in the middle. I couldn't even guess its purpose. His body had well defined muscles and in several places there were interesting designs which appeared to have been painted on his skin. They were fascinating. I had never seen anyone paint colors on their body before. I urged him forward and showed him I wanted him to lean down so I could wash his hair in the pan first.

He seemed to understand immediately. His species must bathe this way sometimes too. We did not waste water like this often, but from time to time we all had to wash our bodies clean of the debris that can build up between our scales and in our hair that become very irritating. I was amazed by how fine his hair shafts were. His hair was thick, wavy and even being encrusted with sand and dried mud it looked so different from our own. The bowl rapidly turned red as the mud came away.

From time to time he would cough. I hoped he wasn't going to become ill from the water still in his lungs. Once his hair was wet and roughly washed I added some of my mother's cleaning soap. It was expensive, but her hair is more similar to this offworlder's than our own. I rubbed the soap in everywhere before having him lower his head so I could wash it out. I then washed his face with one of the rags, water, and a bit of soap. After rinsing I moved on to his chest. I used caution around his brand mark, after I had cleaned his torso I motioned for him to stand. He had already insisted on cleaning his own under arms. It must be a social taboo for someone to touch another person in the underarm area. I would be careful to remember that.

I motioned for him to remove his foot and leg coverings. He paused before he sat on my pallet. He quickly untangled the strange strings on the tops of his foot coverings. His shoes opened wider and he slid his feet out. He wore another layer of coverings under the harder ones. He pulled these off as well. That was when I got a strong smell of his scent. So, his kind has scent markers on their feet. Ours were on our chins. Suddenly I realized what a huge benefit having scent markers on your feet could be. Patrolling would be *MUCH* easier without having to stop and rub one's chin on an object. He would just have to walk along and every step would leave a scent. Incredible! I also found the scent strongly appealing.

He fanned his hand over them and seemed embarrassed to be scent marking my sleeping quarters. I felt a stirring inside that told me that I really liked the idea of his scent being on my pallet.

When he began to shake out the foot coverings I realized just how wet they were. I would have to take his belongings top side to dry them for him. When he released the small disk at the top band of his leg coverings and slid down a small metal piece on a tiny track of metal bits I caught myself wondering how advanced his people really were. He slid the coverings off and shook them out before folding them into a soggy square that he placed on the ground. I knelt at his feet and looked up his body from his extra toes, which were long and thin and had smooth claws like his fingers to his long, lean and slightly hairy legs I was struck again by how different we were.

I motioned for him to remove his loin cloth and as he removed it, I got the shock of my life. I knew my cock was fighting to come out of my slit, but his... was already out. It was semi erect, below hung a strange sack with two large lumps in it. I had no idea what I was looking at.

I felt my own cock breach my slit and I had to adjust myself as it rapidly filled.

I looked up into his stunning eyes and saw a look that I took to be approval. He reached down and wrapped his hand around his own cock. My eyes trailed down his arm to his cock. He wrapped his hands around his cock and began to slowly run it up and down his shaft. My mouth began to water. I saw beads of moisture begin to flow from the slit at the end of his cock. The scent of his arousal made my head spin. Before I could stop myself, I buried my face in the gap between his cock and his thigh. His scent was stronger close to his body. I felt my body strain with need. I reached down and quickly opened my uniform pants. He reached down and pulled at my uniform tunic. I pulled it off and tossed it aside. I struggled to kick off my leg coverings and my loin cloth. They lay forgotten behind me. I reached down and ran my hand over my own straining erection.

While not a virgin, I had little experience with sex play. My society did not frown on it, but being the clawless son of an offworld mother, I was not one that the females sought out. I had been with a few males from time to time, but that was long ago, before I went to the academy. I felt my tail slash back and forth against the floor as I became more aroused. I reached up and carefully ran my hand over his own hand while it stroked his cock. He stepped back so that his feet were on my pallet and pulled me onto my furs.

My eyes went wide. He was willing! I crawled on my hands and feet to him where I felt him pull my body up towards his face.

I thought he was going to press our foreheads together, but instead his tipped my face back and brought our lips together. I instantly froze, suddenly afraid he was about to bury his teeth in my lip. Instead, his lips moved against mine. I moaned and began to try to move mine against his as well. The sensation was incredible! It was a mating of the mouths. It felt so incredibly intimate. I felt my cock pulsing so hard that I began to thrust into the air over him.

I suddenly felt him grasp my cock in his own hand. I jerked in surprise for a moment before I felt his hand begin to slide up and down my length. I moaned into his open mouth. I shuddered with pleasure. His hand was so warm and incredible. His lips were hot and I found myself laying across his heat and rubbing into his cock with my own. He released my cock only to use some of his leaking fluids to rub it over both our cocks. He used both hands to trap our cocks side by side in a tight grip. He then began to move his lips against mine again, stronger and faster. I felt his tongue slide into my mouth and I was lost. He could do anything he wanted to me and

I was going to say I wanted more.

I slid my own tongue into his mouth and felt his lips close around my long, thin tongue and felt him begin to suck at it. My eyes rolled back in my head. I began to frantically thrust into his hand, he slowly removed his hand and I was now thrusting hard into his stomach. I buried my face in his neck when I felt him bring his legs up and wrap them around my hips. I had never had anyone want to take a mating position with me.

I pulled back for a moment and looked at him for confirmation that he wanted this. To my shock, he reached down and began to use his fluids to rub on his back hole.

He motioned like he needed something. Then it dawned on me, he needed sex play lubricant. I pointed to the edge of the furs near the top of the bed. He reached over and lifted the edge. He grabbed the small bottle and I opened it. I offered it to him. He ran his fingers into the thick gel. He then began to run it over his hole before pushing his own fingers in and out of his hole. I leaned back watching him open himself for me. My hand roughly stroked my cock again and again as he worked.

He reached up and grabbed my cock and stroked it several times before nudging my back. He lined my cock up with his hole and rubbed my head around his hole before he urged me to push against his hole. I felt his body open for me. As I slowly pushed in I was shocked by the tight ring of muscles and the heat beyond. I slowly pressed further as my body shook with arousal. Once I was in fully, my head collapsed on his chest. I was inside of the tight, hot hold that I so wanted to dive into again. I concentrated on making my seed come without moving. I opened my eyes, feeling a gentle push on my hip from his foot.

I looked at him before pulling away slowly, I felt so disappointed. I had not managed to release seed. As aroused as I was, it had been too long.

He wrapped his legs around my hips and pulled me back into him. I looked at him confused. He pushed me back again, then pulled me back in close. Oh stars above! He wanted me to enter him again and again! I slowly moved my hips back again and pushed in slowly. He moaned before using his feet to make me move faster. I began to shove into and out of him with more force. The more force I used the higher my arousal got. I ground down into him and he moaned and began to grind his hips into mine as well. The sensation was incredible. I had no idea what those two lumps had been for but I could feel them rubbing near my own hold and suddenly for the first time in my life, I wanted to be filled with a males cock. Not any males, just this male.

I began to thrust into him faster and harder and he

moaned louder before reaching his arms around my chest and pulling us together. He reached down and pinched at the round disks on his chest before he reached back up to take my head and reunite our lips. I felt my breath coming in short pants as I pumped into him as fast as I could. He began to cry out and clutch at my back. I felt his dull nails digging into the thick scales on my back and I felt the need for my seed to be spent. I pulled back and then thrust in again. I was surprised when he pushed my shoulders to the side. He wanted me to roll onto the bed on my back. I thought we must be finished even though I still had not spilled my seed. As we fell to the side, he then rolled so that I was under him and he was crouching over me. He leaned back and began to rotate his hips on mine. I felt my cock bury deeper as he began to thrust against my hips. I felt him shift forward and backward on my cock. I could feel something buried inside of him that my cock was just barely touching.

I cried out in ecstasy as he leaned back so that that inner round spot was being bobbed up and down on. He began to thrust his hand over his cock more and more roughly. I felt my seed begin to travel up my cock. I grabbed him and moved us again so I was leaning over him. I pulled my hips back and slammed them back into him again. I froze in fear that I had hurt him. Instead, he looked at me with the blacks of his eyes now blown so wide there was little of the brilliant color showing. He moaned and I could see his body begin to flush a red color. He cried out and began to meet my every thrust. I ground harder into him before I thrust a couple of times before I felt my body tense. My seed sought his warm depths just as I felt his inner channel began to spasm. He cried out and began to claw at my back in desperation for more.

I slowly slid free of his body with a rush of my seed. I used one of the rags to clean him before I pulled some of my furs from the pile next to the bed. I drew it over myself before I came to lay on his chest. I heard the thumping of his hearts... wait.. Only one thump. He must have only one heart. I put my ear hole over it. I felt him run his fingers through my hair. I looked up at him, my eyes still glazed from ecstasy. He pulled my mouth up and I claimed his mouth again before wrapping my leg around his. I used my tail to stroke his leg. He ran his fingers down my face and I closed my eyes at the pleasure of it. I purred and began to rub my chin across his neck and shoulders. I felt my body tingle and pulse in a strange way I had never felt before. I felt hot and needy. I began to moan and rub myself on him. He kissed me again and started to rub his hands up and down my sides.

I felt my tail arch up and move to the side like I was a female. I couldn't stop the chirps of pleasure when he ran his hand up my tail. He pulled me up on top of him so that I was straddling his waist. I felt my body heat rising as I came to rest on his length. My own cock became hard as a rock again. When he reached to stroke me I cried out and began to rub my hole against his cock. I shook and arched against him. I felt him slide his hand under my body and apply gel coated fingers to my hole. He slid his fingers in slowly and I cried out in both need and a slight fear as well. The more I felt his fingers move inside of me the more aroused I became. I started to raise and lower my body on his fingers. It wasn't enough, I needed more and quickly. I raised off his fingers and reached for his cock. I lined it up with my hole and slowly lowered myself. His cock head was so large I didn't know how it would even fit.

I panted and moaned as I desperately pushed at his cock. I felt it breach through my muscle barrier for the first time and as I slid down his cock I felt the feeling of being filled that I needed so badly. When our hips met, I stopped to look down at him. He ran his hands up my thighs and reached for my cock. The moment he touched it my body arched and my tail became ridged as it bowed over my side. I cried out as I began to sway my hips against his hard shaft. I felt my body spasm as pleasure surged through my core. I rocked back and forth against him as my arousal was driven higher and higher. I needed more and I didn't know what it was I needed. I fell forward and pulled off of his cock. I turned so my back end was pointed towards him. I lowered my chest to the pallet with my back bowed and my tail arched to the side. I knew my hole was open and weeping fluid as he got up and crouched behind me.

I couldn't understand why so much fluid was coming from me, I didn't think he had put that much gel on my hole. I felt him rub his cock against my hole a few times before he pressed into my hole again. I pressed my chest further down and tipped my hips back as he grabbed onto them and began to slowly thrust into my throbbing hole. I cried out and began to pant. My hands clutched at the furs frantically. I tensed and shook as I felt something stirring inside of me. It started as a tiny burst of heat deep in my core. As it grew hotter I felt my body begin to twist and move in strange ways, each more pleasurable than the last. I pressed my face into the furs to hide my ever increasing sounds of ecstasy. I felt the heat into a flame of passion and need that had me ready to explode. I felt him thrust into me fast and hard before he reached under and grabbed my cock. He stroked me in time with his hard thrusts. That was what I needed! I felt my hole clamp down on his cock and begin to pulse with heat and pleasure. He thrust in and out slowly as waves of pleasure crashed over me again and again.

He pulled out as far as he could and slammed into me one more time before he leaned low over my back and I felt his shaft swell before my insides were flooded with his scorching hot seed. I felt it warm its way into my body. I felt like I was suddenly exhausted. As he slowly stopped thrusting, my legs slid out and I collapsed down on my stomach with a moan. He slowly pulled out of my hole and I felt my body pull closed tight. I could still feel the incredible warmth inside of me, tingling its way through me. He carefully cleaned me before he lay behind me. He wrapped his arms around me and held me while I calmed slowly. My tail still felt ridged and I still felt a strong desire. I did not understand how I could still have such a strong need. I have never felt the need to play sex games multiple times to be satisfied. I felt my eyes close as I wondered what that could mean.

CHAPTER FIVE

Sean

I ran my hand across his smooth scales along his lower stomach. Their almost silky feeling was strange but somehow very appealing. I felt his muscles tighten as he began to pant again. I had already seen his cock go flaccid and shrink back into a slit in his groin. No wonder he had been so shocked to see that humans just have it all hanging right out there in full view.

His breathing became more rapid again as he began to moan in low pants. This was now the sixth or seventh time he had gone through this cycle that would end with him becoming frantic for me to take him again. The last time I stepped away from him it only took minutes for him to start to panic and thrash in his sleep reaching for me and crying out. I had no idea if this was a normal reaction for his species or not. The way he was acting reminded me of the time my college roommate got a free kitten and didn't get her spayed. She went into heat for the first time and drove us complexly crazy about it. Perhaps he was in heat?

I was about to try to bring him some relief without hopefully having to have sex again, I was getting both tired and sore at this point when there was a light scratching at the door. I threw a fur around myself and went to the door. His mother stood in the doorway with two bowls that smelled incredible.

"I think there is something wrong with him." I motioned for her to come into the room.

He was already starting to reach for me again while making increasingly frantic mewling sounds. Seeing me near the door caused him to lean out of the furs. He nearly fell from the raised platform. I dove to catch him and rolled him back onto the furs. He moaned and ran his hands over my arms and chest again and again.

I looked back over my shoulder towards his mother. She was hovering near the doorway with her eyes wide. She said something and then hurried from the room. Moments later she returned with a small stone bowl mortar and pestle. She took the bag that he had brought into the room earlier and rummaged through it, pulling out small pouches and dumping them into the stone bowl and pounded it into a powder. She retrieved a small amount of water in a cup and poured the powder into the water and swirled it around until it was well combined. She handed it to me and motioned for me to make him drink it.

He fussed and turned his head, but eventually drank it down as well as the second glass of water she used to get the remaining medicine out of the bottom of the cup. She motioned for me to hold him tight. To run my hands down his skin. She mimicked me pulling him to my chest and putting his head under my chin. He calmed a bit when I held him that way. It felt natural to start to rock with him. It seemed to soothe him more and his breathing calmed as the medicine took effect. He finally calmed enough that he was able to fall asleep in my arms. I slid him down onto the furs and covered him up.

His mother brought me clothing to wear before she left the room. She motioned for me to stay with him. I lay on the furs next to him, watching him sleep. When he would whimper or cry out I would touch him again and he would calm back into sleep again.

A few hours later she returned, this time with a small box in her hand. She came to the furs and knelt down. She opened the box, revealing a small gun like device. As primitive as everything around me looked, I did not expect a high tech looking device. She motioned for me to lean forward and she turned my head. She started to raise the gun towards me and I jerked back. She turned and brushed her rust brown hair back and showed me her own small scar. She spoke quietly and pointed the scar.

I still didn't understand what that was but I guessed it was either some sort of vaccine or something. I leaned forward and she pressed the gun into the side of my head, she moved it around a few times until the thing made a beep, I felt it adhere to my skin, and then she used her other hand to hold my head steady and she activated it.

I felt as well as heard the loud pop. I jerked and flailed. It hurt like I'd just been punched in the head. She laid me back and stroked my hair while I whimpered until the pain started to subside.

"I'm sorry that hurt, I remember it well." She said softly.

My eyes opened wide and I looked at her,

"I understood you!" I whispered.

She grins and nodded, 'Yes, I am sorry it took so long to get back. I had the vender run an update on the software to include any newly acquired species. Thankfully, your species' language is now in the database. Thank you for saving my son's lives. We will be forever in your debt."

"Did the others die from the cold?"

"Yes, they went into shock. None survived, except my

boys. Without you, they would have died. You kept them alive with your body heat."

"That's what I thought." I sighed sadly, "What is happening to him? He was fine and then he started acting.. Strangely. Is this normal for your species?"

"I am like you, an off worlder. I am a different species than my mate. What is happening to him is common among my people. It is a means of adapting to survive. That is part of why we are prized as slaves. We can adapt to most climates and our bodies can adapt physically if necessary. It is not something that happens in his father's species, but he clearly inherited the trait from me. Both of our species form strong bonds with our mates. After we bond, our body's change and adapt to maximize the chances of reproductive success. It appears my son inherited the trait."

"Mates? Wait, did you say to maximize the reproductive success? We are both males."

"Yes?" She looked at me confused.

"Two males cannot reproduce." I said with a laugh that quickly faded, "Are you serious? I could have gotten him... pregnant?"

"Maybe, Maybe not. His body is still going through the process of adapting however, the process requires a large amount of heat to give us the energy to complete the process. We will need to move him topside."

"Like this? How will people react? Especially after what just happened."

"Not well. We would have to travel to one of the remote areas of the city. I have already spoken with my employer. His business is closed for the time being because only sixteen of his nearly three hundred slaves still live. He does not know if he can afford to acquire more."

"Slaves? Was that why I was taken?"

"Yes, the same way I was. We were both rejected from the sale due to defects. First pick always goes to the Royals Caste and they select based on their rank. The next best goes to the high caste. They either buy for personal use or for use in their brothels. They are as picky as the Royals they try to impress so they can make money from the brothels. Next are the merchants. They mostly want slaves for resale purposes or marketing. Next are the laborers. They buy the bulk of the slaves brought here. They become mine workers, sand movers, and stone movers. After the laborers they open up what is left to low caste people, they are mostly food producers and gatherers. They take anything that they deem useful for a purpose.

However, there are a few things that will cause none of them to bid. One of them is defects. In my case, I have a scar here." She touched the scar on her face. "When I was put through the auction, there were lots of slaves for sale but not many buyers. It was also the peak of the gathering season so not many of the lower caste people were there. That meant that I and others like me were branded and abandoned as non-sales. The only way that an unsold slave can survive here is to be mated. Otherwise, no one will give them water or shelter and they die."

"This place is insane!" I gasped.

"It is not like this where you are from?"

"No. Slavery was outlawed centuries ago. No one in my world is legally sold as property, if anyone tries they go to prison for a very long time." I decided not to mention about the illegal sales.

"So how do the businesses have workers? How is your food produced if not for slaves?"

"They choose to accept the jobs or not and they are paid for the work they do. They can leave the jobs if they want."

"Oh, we are paid. The pay is not great, but it is enough to live on. We cannot just leave, though. We do the job because we don't have a choice unless someone like me goes looking for work. Then the person willing to hire them submits a claim and becomes their owner."

"Will I have to do that?"

"Yes. There will be many openings, sadly. What skills

do you have?"

I paused, "Ummm... nothing they would want me for apparently."

"Oh?" She looked at me curiously.

"Do you know what movies are? Recordings?"

"Vids? Yes, of course."

"I was an..." I pause slightly, "actor in vids. I was a performer."

"What did you perform?"

Damn it. I was hoping she would just let that slide. I had no idea how their culture would think of porn. "Well, some people like to watch... intimate videos. Vids of people, being intimate with each other."

"Oh, oh! You were in pornographic vids?"

I turned red and couldn't look at her, "Yeah. I had to drop out of college and had no money. I couldn't find a job, so... I applied with an agency and was accepted. When I was taken, I had finally made it to the top of the best ranked company in the biz. I was on my way to another continent for an exclusive shoot."

"I'm sorry, I'm sure you are very disappointed and angry."

"Disappointed, yeah. I was really looking forward to it. I've wanted to go to London, that's a city in England, for as long as I can remember." I sighed. "Will your son hate me for it?"

"No. He is your mate. He is bonded to you now, he can't hate you. That doesn't mean he won't get mad at you."

"What does that mean? My mate?"

"You do not have mates?"

"We have people who choose to spend their lives together. They get married... or not marry. In theory, they love each other and that keeps them together. That's not always the case."

"So your people do not form the bond?"

"What is that?"

"We lose the ability to breed with anyone else other than our mate, we cannot be separated from them for long or we fall into such deep depression that we may die or take our own lives."

"Shit. Does that mean all the people today that lost their mates...." I waved in the direction of the shelter.

"We will lose many more in the days and weeks to come." Her eyes dropped. "This planet is a harsh place to live."

"Are storms like that common?"

"Storms are common, but not like that one. It will be remembered for generations not only for its duration, force and the amount of its devastation but for the death toll. Much of it was preventable. Maybe now that they have to buy so many new slaves, they will take precautions to keep the slave shelters warm but I doubt it. I doubt it will matter though. Ultimately they just don't care."

I ran my hands over his head and he pressed into my hand, even though he was deeply asleep, "I don't even know his name."

"Your mate's name is De'Ceer. My other son is Relin. I am Fari and their father is Vorel."

"I'm Sean, I'm from Earth."

"Welcome to the family Sean." She smiled at me. "Is Earth a city?"

"No, it's a planet."

"I have never heard of it, or seen anything like you. I did not know any species from our galaxy could produce heat from within."

"Then I'm probably not from your Galaxy. My solar system has nine planets. Do you know of any with nine?"

She shrugged, "I do not know much about space. My area of my home world never had darkness. Not in my lifetime anyway."

"No darkness?"

"No. We have two suns. We are between the two. One very large sun, which we circle and a brighter but a smaller sun that circles the big one. There are five planets between the suns. Only our planet in the middle contains life."

"What about when the planets all form a line between the suns? Wouldn't that cause an eclipse?"

"Yes, but one sun is so big that only part of its light is blocked out. The other sun is so bright that even with the other two planets in the way we could never look that way because it can lead to blindness and if you were on the surface then... you would probably be burned severely."

"I see. So you never saw stars before?"

"No. Not until I came here. I've only seen them a few times. We do not usually go above at night."

"Why?"

"That is when the predators hunt their prey."

"Ah. I see. Makes sense."

"I will leave you to care for your mate. He will get restless again in a while. Try to ease him as best you can. I can't give him the tea for several more hours."

"Could I have already knocked him up?"

"You hit him?"

"No, made him pregnant."

"Yes, you probably already made him gravid."

"Gravid?"

"With eggs.... Don't your people lay eggs?"

"No. I'm a mammal. All mammalians give live birth with like two exceptions and those two are both very strange."

"Then we will find out," she nodded to me and stepped out of the room. I crawled under the furs with De'Ceer and wrapped my arms around him. His skin was cold and clammy. As soon as I took him in my arms, he rolled into me and pressed his body into mine. I felt his arms wrap around me and his tail wrap around my leg. He moaned and grunted as he pressed himself into the heat of my body. I reached for more furs to cover us with. I figured with enough furs on top my body would be able to make him nice and warm without having to go topside.

CHAPTER SIX

De'Ceer

I awoke wrapped in warmth and felt my body tingle with need. I moaned as my cock emerged again. I reached down to stroke myself. I was shocked by how warm I was. Did I fall asleep in the sun again?

That was when I heard a strange sound from next to me. I turned and opened my eyes. The off worlder lay next to me under the furs. He looked so peaceful except for the strange snorting sound coming from him as he breathed. I studied his features as I stroked myself again. I felt my hole clenching desperately again. I had no idea what was wrong with me. I wished he was awake to fill me again. I stroked faster and started to pant with arousal and need. I felt my tail release his leg before going ridged and forcing me to arch my hips into the air with each stroke.

I cried out in frustration. I needed release so badly it

felt like my body was going to tear itself apart. I jerked as I felt his hand touch my stomach. I looked at him, seeing his eyes were awake and rolled over quickly. I moved closer, begging him with my eyes.

He turned and ran his arm over my back before getting to his hands and knees. While still under the covers he slid his body over mine. I moved my hips to the easily position for him and I felt him coat my hole with gel again before he began to slowly push into me. He moved so slowly I wanted to scream in frustration. He pulled at the tops of my knees until I slid my legs down. He tipped my hips slightly so he could still get under my tail as he carefully pushed inside again. My legs were parted wide and the change of position put his shaft at a new place inside of me. I cried out in pleasure as he slowly rocked himself in and out of my hole. He ground himself into my ass at each in stroke. I felt his body lying on top of mine and the feeling of it was astonishing.

I felt my need increasing rapidly, but his pace stayed the same. I started to get frustrated, "Fuck me faster, *PLEASE* fuck my hole. Fuck me. Please fuck me!" I begged him.

As if he understood he rapidly slammed his cock into my hole. The sudden invasion sent shocks of pleasure through me. He slowly withdrew and slammed back in again with more force. I cried out and began to rock myself back and forth meeting his thrusts.

"Yes, yes, my mate. That feels so good. Right there. Fuck me, just like that. Right there!"

He continued to pound the same place until I felt my body tensing, needing more I growled at him. "Fuck me fast and hard, please my mate. I need to come so badly. I hurt! I hurt, please fuck me, make the pain go away!"

He reached around my body before he began to rapidly thrust into me. He began to pound into my ass harder than he had ever done. I felt my body being pushed up the furs with every thrust. He roughly pulled my hips back and pulled my tail up as high as he could push it. I felt him slide it up against his chest and over his shoulder. This position opened my cloaca in a way I didn't know was even possible. I felt him slam into me and hook his hips up at an angle toward my back. I felt a surge of ecstasy unlike anything I imaged could ever exist.

"*THERE! FUCK THERE!*" I roared, "*HARDER*," I cried out as my body shook and tensed. I dug my claws on my hands into the furs to help me push back into my mate. I dug my toe claws into the ground to help lift up higher to meet every thrust. I felt him reach around my body and begin to stroke my cock with hard jerks that went from tip to base in rough movements with his own hips. It felt like I was being fucked while fucking. It was the most mind blowing feeling.

I felt something start to burn inside of me. Like a fire being ignited. It started at the base of my spine and flowed to my testicles. I felt them draw closer to my cock as he pounded in, hitting that amazing spot over over. Every time he did that fire burned brighter. I felt my body tense as the fire moved to condense right on that spot. He hit it again and suddenly the fire burst out through my cock, through my crotch, up my spine, along my skin, to my fingers and toes. Every part of my body was pulsing with extreme pleasure. I held my breath as the sensation continued to pulse through me in waves. I felt my cock shooting spurts of seed out with each pulse.

My mate stroked me harder before he grunted, "I'm gonna come baby, come with me. Come again. Right now!"

The shock that I understood his words was momentary as my body was rocked by even stronger waves of pleasure. I cried out as I felt something inside of me pop. I felt a sharp movement in my lower abdomen and then his cock thrust through something inside of me. I cried out in shock when his heat began to splash inside of me, into a new place. It felt like it was flooding forward towards my belly scales. I felt it warm me and then my body did something it has never done before. I felt it clamp down on his cock in spasms, one after another. I finally collapsed to the puddle on my furs. I felt him lay across my back, struggling to catch his breath.

"Oh baby, oh, that felt so amazing. That was different than before, so different... so good."

"Yes. It was, my mate." I panted, unable to move. When he slowly pulled out he turned me to my back and leaned down over me. He claimed my mouth deeply. I still felt my body shivering with pleasure.

"I am so glad I can finally talk to you, De'Ceer."

"You know my name?"

"I'm Sean. Yes, your mother got a translator for me."

"My mother drugged me," He grumbled.

"Baby, I agree with why she did it. You were too frantic to be calmed even by my taking you again and again."

"I don't know what's happening to me."

"Your mother said you take after her people. That you are going through changes and that you are in heat."

My eyes went wide. No... oh no! Males of my mother's people could spontaneously grow wombs in relationships without a female. Then they can carry offspring like a female. I shook my head. I worked too hard to become and enforcer to become a pregnant male. I would be labeled a defective.

"I can't do this." I tried to push him away.

"I know how you feel. The men of my people don't get pregnant either. We will manage."

"No. I can't. I'm an enforcer! I will lose everything I worked my entire life for." I pushed him away from me. I struggled to my feet, fighting dizziness and threw my clothing on before I struggled to the door. I heard him dressing and following right behind me.

"Son. You cannot leave." My mother stepped in front of me, blocking the door.

"I can't do this! I can't be impregnated like a female! I will be cast out to the sands!"

"We know. Your father and I have a plan. He is already putting it into action. Right now, the city is in chaos. This is likely our own chance. Pack what you can carry, but only what you can hide. Give your mate your hooded cloak. Get ready while I prepare a tea that will hold off your next need cycle for as long as possible."

I nodded. I had a feeling what they had in mind. This was the single most idiotic thing they could have come up with, but it was also likely the only way for us to escape with our lives.

I felt my mate pull me back to my room.

"I think you need to pack quickly. What can I do?"

I looked around, I grabbed my hunting pouches and began to fill them with water packs and dried foods. I packed the few momentos and then dressed my mate in some of my own clothing to help him fit in better. Pulling the hood over his head he almost looked like one of us...

Except for his feet... and the fact that he had no tail. That proved to be an issue with his leg coverings as well. No tail sticking out through the tail opening... meant his rear end was showing. The thought of what I could do with that distracted me for a moment. My mate pulled my pants over his own leg coverings. With my hooded cloak on that wasn't a problem. I grabbed a as many weapons as I thought I could smuggle under our cloak and strapped them to both my mate and I. We carried my entire supply of water and food. I hoped we didn't make sloshing sounds when we walked.

I went to help my mother get my brother ready and dressed. She forced me to gulp down a full cup of her tea. The taste was even worse than the last one and made me gag over and over.

"Drink it. It will stop your heat for a time. I will give you another dose as we are leaving. Don't complain, without it we would not be able to get you and your mate to safety."

I closed my eyes, "Safety? You call this safety?"

"Son, if you do not you and your mate, your brother, your father and I will all be killed. You know that."

I nodded, she was right. We had no choice.

My father walked in the door and nodded at us and motioned for us to follow him quickly. We walked up through the maze of tunnels to the exit that was to the far side of the underground housing area. We exited near the mine where my father worked. It was closed today due to the tragedy. In all its decades of operation, it had only closed three other times. Once was for the honoring the death of our emperor, another was due to a massive cave in, and the only other time was due to the marriage of the owners only son to an offworlder.

Today would be our only chance to escape. We walked quickly through the entrance to the mine and took the lift to the bottom. My father handed each of us a head lamp and we followed him as he led us through the extensive labyrinth of tunnels. Only someone who had been here for nearly every single day of the operation of this mine could possibly know this place as well as my father. He stopped in several places and chipped out some of the precious stones. He filled a sack with them as we went. When that bag was full he handed it to my mother and filled another. We walked for hours through the darkness until we came to what looked like a dead end. My father took some time to scratch and pull at the surrounding rocks until he pulled open a sizeable horde of gems. The rock had been solid. My father gave a chuckle.

"I knew this one would be good. This was my secret."

He tore the gems out and filled the bags by the hand full. We all not carried at least two bags of gems when my father stood and shoved the rocks back. He motioned for us to follow him back down the same tunnel again and we went to what looked like another dead end. That's when he reached behind one of the metal support posts and began to pull on it. It slowly swung open and reveled a narrow hidden passageway. He urged us through and then closed the cover again before running a large number of metal spikes through loops he had pounded into the stone. Now if anyone pulled on the pillar it would not budge at all. He pushed his way past us and led the way down the claustrophobic passage. We dropped lower steadily before coming to a place where the tunnel turned at a right angle and we slide around the bends slowly.

"I put quite a few bends in this part of the passage to hopefully slow anyone who is following us. Don't worry, we are going to make up the lost time ahead. They will be slowed even more by what is ahead.

My father brought us to a stop at an incredibly deep crevasse. He had somehow managed to string up a rope and metal slat ladder.

"One at a time. Eyes straight ahead. Watch your step. Feel with your feet, don't look with your eyes." He showed us how to cross carefully. My brother went next. He tried to act brave but I could tell Relin was terrified. He slowly crossed and then threw himself to the ground and I thought he was going to be sick. Mother went next and she did shockingly well. She felt with her feet, kept both hands on the ropes and her eyes were glued to my father. She carried both of her gem bags and my brothers as well. She made it look easy. I sent my mate next. Even in the darkness I could see that he had gone terribly pale.

"De'Ceer, I'm not good with heights. I... I can't."

"Yes, you can. You're not walking over a height. The ground is only a single hands length under your feet. Look ahead. I brought our lips together. "You can do this. I know you can." He slowly crossed carefully placing each foot. The whole bridge shook with his shaking. My parents helped him up to the wall on the other side where he promptly took the same pose my brother had. I took a deep breath and tried to copy my mother. I felt my heart stutter as the bridge gave a slight drop.

"Son, you need to hurry. Walk quickly. Right *NOW*." I hurried my pace and my father was just yanking me off the bridge when one of the wire support posts on their side pulled out of the rock face. The ramp tipped and left a big gap that could have sent me to my death.

"Well. We made it. Now to remove it." My father untied a rope at the top of each support ring and then he began to pull the rope from where it connected at the bottom below the ramp. The railing rope dropped away and the floor plants now hung in midair on one side. He pulled on the other lower side and as the rope reached the midway point the weight became too much and it rapidly pulled through and the entire floor fell down into the black depths. My father stood and motioned for us to continue like seeing the bridge fall was an everyday occurrence.

"Did you dig this entire tunnel system?"

"Mate of my son, I have been here since I was Rilin's age. I had a lot of time to dig. I was one of the very few willing to work in the deepest reaches. We are territorial down here. We don't let people dig our areas. It's doubtful anyone knows about this area."

"Does it come out somewhere?" My mate asked. I could tell he was getting too stressed. I reached for his hand and gave it a squeeze.

"Yes, it most certainly does, but that is not the end of our journey."

"Oh. Ok." My mate said quietly. I didn't want to tell him that the next part was even worse.

It took a few more hours of walking before we reached a place where my father had chipped hand holds in the wall and it lead up the side of a ledge to where I could see daylight. This was a natural cave that had formed and from the smell of it, was heavily used by the native animals.

"Watch yourselves. They will be sleeping, but they don't particularly like being disturbed."

"What is up there?" My mate whispered.

"It's the sleeping area of a herd of galder."

"What is that?"

"It's a large herbivore. They are very tasty to eat, but they are very difficult to hunt because they travel in large herds and will attack a predator or hunter in masse. They have gotten used to my presence, but they don't know the rest of you. That will make them nervous. Walk outside and wait off to the side behind the boulders while I get my tame ones."

"Tame ones?" I asked my father.

"Yes son, I've spent decades taming many of them and training them to carry heavy loads. You did not think I was going to make us walk across the sands all that way did you?"

"Yes. I did."

"Well, you will just have to trust me."

"I do father, you never cease to amaze me." I shook my head. As we carefully climbed up after him. My mate froze and gaped in disbelief.

'Dinosaurs?! You have fucking dinosaurs here?!"

"You know what they are?" I whispered in surprise.

"Yes! They evolved on my home world hundreds of millions of years ago only to be wiped out by a meteor."

My parents gaped at him in shock.

"Your home world? They are from your home world?"

I nodded, "We have fossils that you can see them

evolving slowly over time. You can even see fossilized foot prints too. They died out millions of years ago on my world! I was obsessed with them as a child. I think we call them a plateosaurus, or I think it's a more evolved version of it at least. Its head is much larger than the ones I saw in books, its feet are different too.

"They have had a lot of time to change." My father whispered.

My mate walked carefully through the herd just in front of me. The herd all got to their feet and looked at us carefully. When we settled behind the boulders my father when back in and soon came out leading several on ropes tied around their necks. He had also fashioned a sort of pad over their back for us to sit on. He singled them to lay down and helped us each up onto their backs before handing us the ropes.

My father mounted the largest one and used the rope to turn its head toward the open desert. As we started off, most of the herd came along. I looked at my mate who was grinning widely. I think for my mate this was all his childhood dreams coming true. I couldn't believe my father had tamed them. As far as I knew no one had ever tried.

We rode until the heat became too much and my father let the beasts hurry us to the nearest cave. This one had a small pool of water in the back. It was well used by animals, but it was moving well enough that it was fairly clean. Most of the inhabitants of the cave ignored our presence. I realized it had to be because they didn't see us as anything other than an extension of the beasts. When they lay down to rest we lay beside them for safety and so we could mount quickly.

My mate was petting his galder when it suddenly jerked its head around. I could tell by its reaction something was wrong.

"Mount now!" My father whispered. We all climbed on just as we saw movement near the front of the cave. Many of the animals began to back away. Some making threatening displays.

"What's going on?" Sean asked.

"I'm not sure," my father answered. "This isn't how they react to a predator, but something has them very unhappy."

The animals began to push at each other as they crowded away from the entrance of the cave. Some bolted out the door. My father told us to lean down low and hold on tight. Our galder charged forward with a burst of speed. I glanced at my family to make sure they were all still holding on. I felt my beast swerve and I looked to see what they were avoiding. I saw a landing craft parked around the edge of the dune. Fucking hell! Of all the times to have some royals and high caste decide to come out to hunt or just mess around with the wildlife.

We kept as low as we could as we continued on with the mass of animals through the heat. I knew this was not ideal. I worried about what being out in the heat would do to my soft skinned mate. He already looked very red and burned. My mother was getting overheated as well.

My father let the herd lead us to the next oasis. By the time we arrived, the cave was already very crowded. The animals pushed their way inside until there was very little room to even breathe. My mate was wiping sweat from his face.

"Drink water. You are losing far too much water, mate."

How long will this trip be?"

"About five nights."

"So... six days?"

"About."

"We don't have enough water for me for even a few days. I obviously require far more water than you guys."

"We will fill up on water where the animals go. It's not ideal, but it will keep us alive."

"Will it be safe to drink? Are their waterborne diseases, parasites, or other nasty things?"

"As long as it is free flowing, then no."

My mate looked tired, but he was a bit better by the

time the worst of the heat was over. I on the other hand, could feel another heat surge coming on fast. Thankfully, my mother had already prepared the teas and had it in a sealed pouch which she passed to me. I gulped it down then tried not to lose it again. My mate drank three pouches of water, my brother a half pouch, and my parents both got a pouch. I could tell that my mate needed more, but was afraid to drink it.

"At the next stop you will drink more. Understand?"

He nodded as the beasts began to carefully walk out of the cave my father spotted something in the distance that made him curse. There was a figure watching us from the top of the next dune. We were being followed. My father let the beasts amble slowly over the next rise and then spurred his beast on. The whole herd followed as we hurried across the open dunes. I had no clue how my father could possibly have spent so much time out here and still managed to check in and out every day and make his quota as well. My father was amazing.

The beasts finally slowed as night approached, they had brought us to a grazing area. This would be a very dangerous time. The beasts had to feed, but this was where the predators came to hunt.

"Be on the lookout, weapons at the ready. Relin, you will ride with me," my father motioned for him to bring his beast closer and he climbed in front of my father. As the night plants emerged from their tubes the beasts grazed on the bioluminescent plants. This world seemed like two separate worlds. By day it was bone dry and appeared to have no life anywhere. However, at night the hidden life bursts forth with reckless abandon on the quest to survive.

I could hear the sound of predators calling in the distance and our beasts hurried away from the sound. They were alert but did not seem overly concerned. My mate was a nervous wreck. Apparently his night vision was extremely poor. His fear was making his best nervous. Eventually I managed to get him to calm down by moving him to my beast. This was not good if my beast had to run fast, but my mate finally relaxed. Just as the night was approaching my mate turned and gasped then started to kick at my beast whose head shot up. It saw what my mate did and bolted forward nearly unseating me.

"*GO!*" screamed my mate and in one swift move my father had the whole herd running away as fast as they could go. Our beast was too slow carrying two, I steered it towards my mates which had stayed close. I jumped between the two and we began to make up the time. Glancing back, I was shocked and dismayed to see how close the predators were. If we did not find a way to speed them up we would all be killed.

My father yelled to take our beasts into the main herd. It meant risking that they might fall, but ultimately it might save our lives.

There was a screech as one of the slower members of the herd was attacked. It went down hard and a few of the fast moving predators were distracted by kill. However the rest still followed us in fast pursuit. We came over the next rise and my father cursed. The same caravan of royals and high born was now parked, having a damned meal in the middle of our escape route. The heard swerved to avoid the screaming people, but some were mowed down and fell under the herd. Others made it to the safety of their transports. The predators were on them in a moment. They stood no chance at all. I glanced over my shoulder and watched in horror as the predators decimated the camp and all in it. Even the transports gave little protection to their occupants. As we reached the top of the next dune. The herd slowed. They were heavily winded. They walked slowly, trying to catch their breaths.

"Oh my God," my mate said. "All those people!"

"I know, mate. To make matters worse, those were royals and high caste people."

"Will they try to blame us if they catch us?"

"Probably, but in truth, we had no idea they were there. Likely it won't matter."

My father pointed. I spotted what looked like the same figure walking back toward the royals camp, "Oh no.. If he goes back there he will be killed." He turned his beast and we rode toward him slowly. My father raised both of his hands and called out that we mean no harm.

He pulled up in front of a male whose cloak and amulet showed him to be the fourth son of the emperor. My heart stopped.

"What are you doing out here, slaves?"

"You cannot go back there, royal. Our herd was chased by predators. Your camp was in the middle of the game trail."

The male went pale, "I told them! I fucking *TOLD* them not to put camp there. My father refused to listen to me!" His breathing quickened. "Did you see..."

My father nodded and bowed his head, "I'm sorry. There are likely no survivors and the predators will likely be following the herd. You will have no chance of escaping them on foot."

"Was the High Emperor at that encampment?"

The males face went still before he nodded. He blinked his eyes rapidly. "Everyone was. The whole royal family and the highest ranked of the high born. They were celebrating the mating of my second brother. They brought the camp out here because they said the sound of all the wailing and carrying about was annoying them."

He turned his face away and I could tell that those words were not his own.

"Ride my brother's galder. He can ride with my mother," My mate pointed to my brother.

The male nodded, "I take it you won't be heading back to the city?"

"No, we will not. But if you go back that way, neither will you. Ever." My mate told him with a stern look. "You have two choices. Come with us now, or stay behind. This delay is giving the predators time to catch up."

He nodded and went to the galder who, thanks to my father's training automatically lay down for him to climb up on its back.

"How was this done? I never thought it was possible to ride them."

"Necessity breeds invention," my mate said simply before turning his beast away.

"Yes, that it does." The male clung to the beast as we had the first few hours. We hurried to catch up with the herd as they walked toward their next resting place. It took a few more hours to reach it, but thankfully it was not very crowded. The water source was clean and fresh and flowed out of a crack in the wall and along the end of the cave before going back down into the rock through another crack. My mate drank cup after cup of water. He drank until I was afraid he was going to get sick.

I filled up all of our water pouches, even the ones that had contained my tea. I to surprise, and concern, my heat had not returned.

You still do not require more tea, son?" She asked quietly.

"No mother, I feel fine."

My mother sighed and I knew she was upset. I guessed she was upset that I had already conceived before she got the tea to me. The only way that I was not in heat already was if I had already conceived.

I looked at my mate as he leaned on his beast. They both slept soundly. My species only require a few hours of sleep at a time and typically we sleep in the heat. We left my mate to sleep inside and went out to bask.

"What is your name?"

"I'm De'Ceer and the off worlder is my mate, Sean."

"I am Yarlorn, I guess I'm the emperor now if everyone else is dead. I need to get back to deal with the fall out of this. I won't send anyone after you."

"Frankly, I would rather send you back, but how do you propose we do that?"

"I could take that one and head back on my own."

"You could try, but it would never leave the herd," my father sighed. "There is a remote outpost one more days ride away. We can leave you there and you can call for help."

"Where will you go?"

"Like we would tell you?" I snapped.

"De'Ceer, stop. He is not being rude to you. Don't be rude to him. Have some compassion, he just lost his entire family."

"Actually, I am more upset about the fact that the remaining royals and high born will be scrambling all over themselves to take over the empire as soon as word spreads."

"You are not upset about your family?" I asked.

He paused before slowly shaking his head, "I'm not like them. Never was and they knew it, too. I was an outcast in my own family. They couldn't get rid of me, but they didn't want me either."

"Ah, the struggles of the rich and famous, which to take out today... the Bentley or the Lambo... such problems," My mate said from the mouth of the cave. He was leaning on the wall with his arms crossed.

"What does that mean?"

"It means you think you have problems? Try being a slave! Slavery is sick, evil, and the worst sort of depravity and yet you complain that you have problems."

"What's wrong with slavery?"

"Spoken like someone who owns other people."

"I don't own slaves."

"No, no.. You just benefit from them."

"I don't understand," he sat up and turned around to face my mate.

"You want to understand? Here goes: On my planet slaver was abolished centuries ago. Yet... I was walking down the street on my world and I got shot in the back by some really creepy totally identical men. They then locked me in a small wire cage with a bunch of other people. Once every cage in the truck was full we were taken to a warehouse and brought up a ramp, slid into a solid metal box... that solid metal box was then *SLOWLY* filled with water so cold it burned like fire. I was paralyzed and could do *NOTHING* as the water slowly trickled into my nose and mouth and filled my lungs. I could do *NOTHING* as I was frozen alive. Then.. I was brought here. Unthawed... publicly examined, and had this *BURNED* into my chest." He raised up his shirt and showed the still seeping wound which looked angry and was probably now infected. Oh?? Was that all? No. No... I was thrown out onto the hot sand in the middle of the fucking day and nearly cooked alive... while.. Ironically, still being partially frozen. Still paralyzed, of course. I had some child grab me by the foot and drag me around trying to get their parent to let them keep me... or that was just my take on it. The parents made them leave me on the side of the road where a short time later a *MASSIVE* sand storm hit and I felt myself being slowly covered in sand and being suffocated. Thankfully De'Ceer saved my life by taking me to the slave shelter. When I was finally able to move when the storm was over? When I could finally look around? Dead bodies. A sea of *HUNDREDS of DEAD BODIES*. I was in a room full of corpses. Why? Because no one gives a shit if slaves freeze to death... they are replaceable right? Just go and steal some more, right? Well, guess what? Every one of those people are now being mourned. That wailing your precious relatives were so annoyed by... was the sound of people mourning their loved ones. And now. I am trapped on a planet where people are disposable goods. A planet where people are not treated with respect and where life is not treasured. I always thought that if there were aliens out there, then they must be advanced enough that we could learn from them. I guess I was wrong. You people aren't more advanced. You're primitive barbarians with fancy toys that I doubt you invented yourself. As far as I'm concerned. You should have been left to the predators. Anyone who believes they have the right to own another sentient being is not worthy of my respect. Respect is earned, not commanded." My mate turned and walked back into the cave. Turning your back on a member of the royal family, or any of the things he just said to the new emperor could get him killed. I looked at my parents who genuinely looked afraid for my mate.

The emperor rose and walked after him. He held up his hand as I tried to follow, "It's actually refreshing to hear someone not tell me what they think I want to hear."

"Wait," he called after my mate, who refused to respond.

"What do you mean you were stolen from your world? Nothing that you described is how things are done here."

"Yes, it is. What he described is exactly what happened to me as well." My mother said sadly. She revealed her brand as a rejected slave.

"But what about your contract? You agreed to the terms when you signed up."

My mate gaped at him blankly. "What fucking contract. I didn't agree to any contract. What part of '*I was shot in the back while walking home?*' sounds like I agreed to this at any point?"

"There are no contracts." My mother agreed. "We are stolen from our worlds by force and then sold at the auctions."

"But you were paid up front, to compensate your families for your time here...." The emperor looked confused.

We all laughed.

"Paid? You think we were paid before being brought here? No way. Our families have no idea where we are! They likely think we are dead." My mother said, crossing her arms over her chest.

"We pay the brokers large sums of money to acquire people. They are supposed to hire people willing to come here. Then people buy their contracts at the auction house based on how much they are willing to pay for that person's service. They work the number of years indicated in the contract and then they can leave."

"I was stolen from my home world when I was my son Relin's age." My father told him, "I have five more years left on my contract. I have black lung already. How many people do you think live long enough to pay back their contract cost? Not many, I can assure you. Not one of the people that were sold to the mine along with me are still alive. I'm the last. I have never heard of a single person ever leaving once they come here. Not one. Once here, we die here."

"But, the pay.."

"What part of *'slave'* says paid well?" I asked him. "My father has a quota that is enough that most miners work as hard as they can just to reach... and if they don't... no water! If they go above quota... they can get a tiny amount of money... just enough to put food in the belly and if they get really lucky.. Manage to save up for a place to live. We were lucky and my father has a damn good eye for mining. He is one of their top earners. We had a nice home. For most... there is no home. It means sleeping in the walkways, or cramming together forty or more to a room. Slaves are treated with no respect at all. We are used, we are abused, and we are thrown away or killed when we do not make their quotas or are no longer needed. My wife and I had two other children. They were both stolen from us at birth. Where do you think they went? No place good is my guess. They may have been killed. Slavery only benefits those who profit off the business. Do you think I did not hear the way you demanded to know where we were going? How you said 'slave' with a sneer? You think that is not exactly what we expect from someone like you? You wouldn't have offered us any aid at all if the roles were reversed. But we brought you with us to save you. I guess that's the difference between us. We value people's lives, you only see peoples value if it has a monetary benefit to you." My father turned and walked back out into the sun. He lay down on the rock and closed his eyes. I have never been prouder of him than I was just now.

"I always looked up to my father because he's a strong man. He works hard to provide for us and he's a really good person." My brother said quietly. "But to you, he's just an old slave with dulling claws. Do you think the mine cares if he gets black lung? Or gets hurt? Do you think they would care about us if he dies? No. I wanted to work in the mine, so badly, to help him bring in money so that he didn't have to work so hard. But it wouldn't have mattered. He would still have had to work just as hard because of the quota. I've watched most of my friends get sold off already. The only reason I wasn't sold off already was because I have bad claws. I would never make quota. I have no value to them. I'm surprised they didn't kill me as a hatchling." My brother turned to join my father.

"I worked hard to fight for the right to become an enforcer. I'm the first slave to do anything other than a purely slave role. But, I was not treated as anything other than a slave. I'm well aware that allowing me to be an enforcer was a token gesture. I was only allowed to patrol the market place, but I was given no actual authority to do anything. I'm not even *ALLOWED* to stop, question, or arrest anyone unless they are a slave. How many slaves do you think shop at the inner city market spaces? None. My brother and I would have died at the slave shelter because we would never have been allowed into the warriors shelters, even though I am an enforcer. I fought to give people like my brother a chance for better things.... But even I know it was a waste of time and nothing I have ever done has changed a demand thing so long as I am a slave." I turned and walked to my mate who took my hand and lead me back to the mouth of the cave. I could still hear my mother talking to the Emperor inside. I doubted anything that we said would matter to him. My mate sat resting in the shade just inside the cave as I basked on the sand. My head was still swimming with things I should have said, but ultimately it didn't matter. Nothing that I ever did made a difference anyway.

CHAPTER SEVEN

Sean

I was surprised to hear the rest of De'Ceer's family speak their minds. Judging from the look on that royal's face, it was the first time anyone did that. He didn't react badly, he just looked stunned. I think he honestly believed that we had been paid to come here. Seriously though? How naive can a person be? The very word *'slave'* refers to someone being bought and sold against their will. When he finally came outside again, he sat off on his own. He kept staring at his amulet like it had all the answers. I started to feel bad for him. Maybe he really was grieving for his family and just hadn't shown it yet.

I finally got up and went to sit next to him. I didn't say anything at first. I gave him time to decide if he was going to talk or not.

"I don't think I care that they are dead."

"Your family?"

"Yes," he said quietly, 'but it breaks my heart hearing about how many slaves died. People who had no choice about coming here. People who were killed by the sheer negligence of people like my own family and by extension.. Me."

I nodded, there was nothing I could say. He was right. Telling him all was forgiven wasn't my right.

"I was lied to. Every single thing they ever taught me was a lie. People don't throw the festivals to honor us out of being grateful to us for everything we have given them do they?"

"I just got here, but I seriously doubt it." I said quietly.

He looked over the dunes ahead of us, "I'm the emperor now, but I have no idea what to do."

"Then do things right, end the suffering of innocent people just to make money."

He blinked before nodding, "How? There will be so much resistance from the slave owners."

"Do the same thing our president did, abolish slavery regardless of if they agree with it or not. Granted, we had a civil war over it, but ultimately the slavers lost because more people wanted to be free than those who wanted to keep them captive? Then, give them the choice to return to work for fair pay or to start their own business and to run their own lives. Some of the greatest inventions on my world that are still used today, came from freed slaves. Once freed, many turned their lives around with hard work and ended up very well off because of it. Not all did so great, but that's life. You win some, you lose some.

It's not an easy to survive here. Obviously. Life is a daily struggle. But how much more could you accomplish with a population which has been enabled to do more than just shove around rocks? Look at what one man accomplished because his family needed a faster and safer way across the desert." I pointed to De'Ceer's father. "I was told no one had ever through to try to tame these beasts before. Now, the dunes are not such a threatening barrier. Domesticating those animals means a stable food supply, a means of transportation, and labor."

The man nodded, "The benefit of them did not escape me. I agree with everything you said. I believe if I do this, there will be civil war here, like on your world. I will likely pay for it with my life."

"Then you would be a martyr. Like Abraham Lincoln was," I said quietly.

"He was killed?"

"Yes, he was shot in the head while at a theater. He is remembered as one of our greatest presidents for being willing to give his life to bring about the changes that, long after his death, brought our country into being one of the greatest powers on our planet. There is far more to everything than that. However, his taking a stand against slavery might have made him very unpopular among the slave owners, but he was a hero and an inspiration to the rest." I reached into my back pocket, and fished around to pull out my wallet. I had kept it even though most of its contents were now useless or destroyed. I opened it up and fished around in the depths of the folds until I fished out some change. I handed him a penny. "That's him. His face is on every penny."

He took the coin and looked at it, "What is this?"

"It's money. The smallest denomination of money we have, but it is also the most numerous. It used to be worth far more than it is now, but he was one of the greatest presidents we had."

He went to hand it back to me, "Nah. You keep it. I think you need it more than me. When you feel like you don't know what to do, think about what he would have done."

He closed his fingers around it tightly.

"Thank you," he said quietly.

I began to thumb through my wallet, most of its contents were ruined. I came to a picture that I had laminated long ago. I looked at it and sighed.

"Who are they?"

"My family."

"They must miss you terribly."

"No. They don't. My parents were…. Deeply religious. They believed so strongly in what they were told by their religious leaders that it completely overruled their common sense. They were brainwashed into thinking that their God hates all gay people. People who like the same gender: men who love other men or women who love other women. So, when they found out while I was in college that I had been living with another man who wasn't just my roommate... well. They disowned me. They cut me off completely. I was told to never contact them again for any reason what so ever. I was told that I was possessed by an evil demon and until I cast out, that the evil sin of being gay, then I would never be allowed near them again."

"How does a man being attracted to another man mean another person has been taken over by a demon spirit?"

I laughed, "Exactly. They stopped paying for my college education. I was left with no money, no place to live, no job, and nowhere to go. The boyfriend I was living with decided to move back in with his parents and we stopped seeing each other. I would have been homeless if I hadn't seen an advertisement looking for people to audition... for pornography. I spent the last of my money to travel half way across the country for the audition. If I had not been hired, I would have been sleeping under a bridge that night. Well... actually I did that anyway until my first paychecks came in." I sighed. "I think the fact that I was making so much money doing something that would infuriate my family beyond all reason... was part of its appeal."

I heard him start to chuckle, "That's what I was just thinking as well. You and I are similar in that. I never got along with my family. I didn't like the way they treated others and when I stood up for people I was treated badly for it. Now I understand why they did it. They wanted to make themselves feel more important and to keep the ones they were targeting from thinking they were worthy of being treated with respect. I think I knew that all along." He looked down at the penny in his palm, "I know what I have to do. Thank you Sean, no matter how this turns out, know how much I respect you and your family.... De'Ceer's family that is." He laughed a little before his head jerked to the side. I saw him shade his eyes from the sun.

"What is it?"

"Approaching air craft. Heading this way. I think they are following the tracks of the herd."

"Shit! We have to go."

"No. If you flee I can't protect you. Go tell your family

to do everything that I say. *HURRY.*"

I scrambled to my mate and told him what was happening. We mounted our beasts and waited for the aircraft to approach. The herd bolted away from the terrifying sound of the aircraft as it landed, but we were able to keep ours from running with them.

Numerous heavily armed males charged out of the aircraft, aiming heavy weaponry at us.

"*HOLD YOUR FIRE!* That's an *ORDER.*" Bellowed the emperor.

The men all froze but did not lower their weapons.

"You will stand down immediately. You are threatening the people who saved my life. I owe them a life debt."

"Emperor Yarlorn, they are runaway slaves!"

"They are not slaves anymore. They are free. They risked their own lives to save mine. I will not allow them to be mistreated in any way. Is that understood?"

The leader of the troops bowed deeply to the emperor before he stood and directed his men to secure the area.

The emperor came to me and smiled, "Just stick with me and I will to my best to make sure you are all treated well."

"Thank you, Emperor." De'Ceers mother said and bowed deeply from where she sat on her beast.

"All of you can call me Yari, please, I would like that

very much."

He looked at me and I could see the emotion in his eyes.

"Okay, Yari, care to go for a ride?" I asked and lead up the best he had ridden earlier.

"Yes, I do, I hope you will return with me and bring these wonderful animals along as well. I really do need to have people I can trust around."

I looked at the others and we all nodded in silent agreement.

He smiled and nodded.

As we ambled past the shocked looking troops we just grinned. I couldn't help but laugh as the troops poked at each other and pointed. Yes. I am in fact... riding a dinosaur. I couldn't help but wonder how long it would take before the whole population were going to be riding like this? I also need to explain how a horse cart or a buggy worked. I had a feeling that they would become incredibly popular here as well. I couldn't help but notice the way some of them glared at us. They would love nothing more than to shoot us right now. Yari was right, if he did send us on our way we wouldn't live to see the next sunrise.

CHAPTER EIGHT

De'Ceer

I helped my father coax the skittish beasts into the flyer. My mate had told us to cover their eyes and ear holes so that they would be calmer. He said it worked on his world with frightened animals. They did settle down once they were blindfolded, but it still was not easy to coax them into the belly of the craft. The pilot said it would be a tight fit and we would be pushing the maximum carrying capacity of the flyer, but he thought it was possible to transport them... so long as we kept them calm and quiet. Sure. No problem!

The troops kept their distance from the beasts which helped, but surprisingly Yari was right there with us. He had really fallen for the female he had been riding. My father told my brother he would tame him a new one when my brother protested. Take off was a bit rocky, but it evened out and the beasts stayed remarkably calm as long as they could touch each other. The flight was short and as I watched us fly over the mine, I realized I was right back to where we started in the same position. I was still gravid. I was still going to be in danger no matter what. My only option was to stay on Yari's good side and hope he can get us to safety.

I had spent the time I was basking thinking about what was bothing me about my relationship with Sean at this point. Other than I was just getting to know my mate, I realized that I had just somehow thought I would be the dominant partner. I thought I was going to be the strong protector. Now... I was still the bigger of the two of us and clearly I was physically stronger... but I now carried our young and my mate who I should be protecting was now going to have to protect me. I realized that I was feeling confused and a bit frustrated because I didn't know where I stood now. I told myself that he and I would talk about it when we had the chance. Right now, in the belly of a flyer surrounded by royal guards, enforcers who now looked at me like they were planning my death was not the time. Actually, they probably were planning my death for abandoning my post and for being a runaway slave. I had to protect my mate and our unborn as well as my family somehow.

With a slight thump the flyer landed in the middle of an expansive enclosed stone courtyard. I had never seen what was on this side of the stone wall. Only the royals, select high caste, and their guards were allowed through the inner gates. One more stone wall rose up in the distance. That was the Imperial household, only the Emperor, his family and their staff, servants, and personal slaves were allowed in. A throng of people stood in a massive line many people thick awaiting the return of their new Emperor.

"Alright, let's make a good entrance." Yari laughed and jumped up on his beast and swung his leg over.

We slowly rode out, giving our beasts time to look around at the unfamiliar scene. There was no sense in hurrying them and ending up clinging to them as they panicked and ran. Once back on solid ground they relaxed slightly. Yari led the way past the rows of people up to the best dressed of the lot. A cluster of males stood looking unamused at our entrance.

"Emperor Yari, we had assumed you were deceased. Imagine my surprise when I find you had been found consorting with... runaway slaves? Please tell me these criminals kidnapped you. I will have them executed immediately." One of them said with a sneer of disdain, looking at my father.

"These fine people saved my life. I would have been dead right along with the rest of my family if not for them risking their own lives to save mine. I owe them a life debt. I strongly suggest you keep that in mind if you should ever think of expressing a desire to hurt any of them again." Speaking loudly, "This family saved my life. I owe them a life debt! They will be treated with respect at all time. They will not be threatened or mistreated. They are under my care and protection. Is that *CLEAR*?"

Seeing Yari go from the quiet, soft spoken man I had watched talking with my mate just a few hours ago to this strong and honestly a bit intimidating man was... shocking.

"Yes, Emperor," the entire crowd of thousands suddenly bowed.

"Gather all people in the courtyards immediately. Sound gathering bells," he told the man in the fancy clothing.

"Yes, Emperor Yari." He bowed and hurried off.

Next we were approached by a finely dressed female who asked the emperor if he would like to be changed and refreshed before he was seen publicly. To my surprise, he refused.

"People will see me as I am," he told her simply and she bowed and backed away slowly.

Several more people approached him, each acting fearful and bowing. Was this how the royals were normally treated?

Finally a young slave girl dressed in nice clothing

approached with a tray of food and an entire pitcher of water she knelt down and placed the tray on a small disk that was woven into her hair. My stomach turned. The emperor was to use this little girl as a table while he ate. Even the thought of it made me sick. Was this what had become of my older brothers? Had they become like this girl?

Yari had clearly seen this before. He passed the food around to us and we ate quickly. There were many people gaping openly as Yari openly served slaves with food from his own plate. He then shared his water with us as well. The food was better than anything I had ever eaten in my life. There was not a trace of the grit of sand in it at all.

He then dismissed the little girl who hurried away with the tray held in front of her. He stepped closer to us and whispered quietly, "That is one of the many things that will change."

"Thank you," I whispered back just as the gathering bells began to toll. It would take time for everyone to be assembled. When he called everyone, he meant everyone. That meant that the people down in the mining pits had to be called up from the depths as well.

"Emperor Yari, I am so glad to see that you are safe!" A woman in a long fancy gown came running forward.

"Yes cousin, I am safe. For once, I am very glad that

you stay out of public gatherings." Yari greeted her warmly.

"I have been told of the tragedy, it is too horrible to even think of. How did you survive? I was told there were many predators."

"I had gone to the top of one of the dunes, some distance away to watch the movement of the herds on the other side of the narrow passage. I could see down the passage, but not back into the camp. I saw the herd of animals coming toward me, and thankfully these fine people who were riding some of the beasts stopped and rescued me. The predators were not far behind. If I had stayed I would not be here. There was nothing I could have done. I could hear what was happening in the distance, which was why I was heading back to camp. I *TOLD* him that was not a safe place to make camp, cousin. I *TOLD* him that predators hunt along the game trails through the desert, but he wouldn't listen."

"Oh, Yari. I'm so sorry. I know he wouldn't have listened to anyone and no one would have dared do anything other than his order. I saw his reckless behavior on the dunes as a child. That was why I refused to go, not after I too was nearly taken when I was a mere child. Sadly, this does not shock me. I think he thought he could command the predators to eat someone else instead."

Yari smiled sadly and nodded, "I believe you are right cousin. I would like you to meet the people who saved me."

We all introduced ourselves to Yari's cousin and she thanked each of us in turn for saving Yari. Unlike the cold reception we received from everyone else, hers was warm and friendly.

"Cousin, I am now the emperor and am about to announce many changes. Some are likely to cause some of the population to become enraged. I think it would be best if you left the city for a time. I do not want anything to happen to you."

"What are you going to do?"

"You will find out soon. But please, understand that it is the right thing to do and that it must be done. Even if some of the people resist it, even if I ultimately pay with my life, I am doing this because it is morally right. Even if I am killed for the changes I want to make, please continue to fight for these changes. No matter what, please?"

"Yari, you're scaring me," she said quietly.

"I know, my sweet cousin." He reached up and trailed his fingers down her face, "this will be the start of a very difficult time for all of us, but I want this world to be a place we can be proud onto our own children. I do not want to continue a society that runs based on lies."

She looked confused, "Lies? What lies?"

"Everything we were told growing up, all of it, it was lies."

She went pale, "Please tell me simply."

"The slaves. They are people who are captured by force against their will. They are brought here and sold with no agreement. They are held against their will and severely mistreated or killed if they stand up for themselves. The storm that killed 'some of the slaves' as we were told, killed everyone in the slave storm shelter except for three of these people. That's hundreds of people in that one shelter alone. I already asked, the same thing happened in all of them. The death toll is over four thousand people already."

She gasped and covered her mouth, "I asked, I was told it was only a few who didn't make it to the shelters."

"I believe we are being told nothing but lies. It is time for the truth to be known by all."

"They are really stolen from their homes?" She turned to look at us.

"I was shot in the back while walking home from an important awards party." My mate began, "I most certainly was not asked if I wanted to be a slave. I was not paid. I was paralyzed by whatever they shot me with, put in a cage, then into a solid metal box and it was flooded with icy water until I drowned. I awoke to being dumped out on a table, examined and found lacking. I then had a brand burned into my chest and was dragged by my leg outside to burn in the sun and to die from the approaching sandstorm. I have since learned that this is the routine treatment people receive here."

"The same happened to me too. My mate took me in and gave me his own water supply to keep me alive until I could find someone willing to take a contract with me as a slave. I had to settle for half slave cut. I make half the amount the rest of the slaves do. My husband has to make up the difference."

"Half rations?" Yari's brows furrowed.

"Yes, that is typical for people like us."

"We were rejected for our faults." She touched her missing eye and the scars on her lip. "I will never understand why I was taken in the first place, why take someone that clearly no one here would buy?" My father wrapped his arms around my mother.

"Fate," he whispered, "it was fate that brought you to me, my love."

Yari smiled softly, "This is some of the wrongs that must be brought to right. No matter what the cost."

She nodded, "Yes, cousin, I agree. I will support you."

"Emperor Yari, the people are gathered. Including the miners and the gatherers who were asleep."

"Yes, Garen. Please see that there are as many guards

as possible on the walls. Close the gates now."

The advisors brows furrowed in confusion, "Yes Emperor Yari." He hurried off to carry out the orders.

"Alright. Let's hope we can keep we can keep the chaos to a minimal," he whispered.

He bowed his head and took deep breaths, trying to calm himself. I walked to him and put my hand on his shoulder. One by one each of my family and his cousin joined him. My mate leaned into me and I slid my arm around his side.

Yari slowly raised his head and nodded slowly. We stepped aside and he led us to a stone platform I saw the microphones that would broadcast his words to all people of our city. I knew that this would be one of the hardest things Yari had ever done and I had to give him credit. His balls must be bigger than mine because I was scared, not only for him but for all of us.

"The old emperor has fallen," Yari began. For most this was the first they had heard of the death of the emperor.

"My father led by cruelty, callousness, and a complete lack of compassion. He would listen to no one. He would take the advice of no one, and it was that lack of ability to listen to others that cost him and almost the entire royal family their lives."

There were gasps throughout the city. The murmuring

picking up until Yari raised his hand.

"In this time of great sorrow, when so many were mourning the loss of over four thousand of our people, my father decided that he was too annoyed at hearing the sounds of mourning. He decided to take the entire royal family out into the open desert to celebrate a marriage arraignment he had made. He started off the day by chasing a whole herd of animals out of their shelter and away from their water source so he and his concubines could go frolic in the water. Bathe in it... and urinate in it."

Yari paused to allow the shouts of anger to die down. It was a death sentence to abuse a water source. Hearing that the Emperor himself had done it infuriated people, and rightfully so.

Yari raised his hand again.

"He then tired of his sport and had the flyers take him and his party to another location. I warned him strongly that the location was not safe. It was in the middle of a game trail and near a water source. He did not listen to my warning. When I left the camp to observe the movements of the animals down the passage between the rifts, I heard screaming in the direction of the camp. I turned to return to camp. I saw a herd charging in my direction. Upon the backs of a few of the herd were people. They stopped their beasts and told me not to go back that way. That there were predators everywhere. They told me that if I stayed I would be killed. There was no way that I could escape on foot. I rode one of their beasts away from the predators. I could still hear the predators. They were far from quiet. There was nothing that I could do. I was unarmed.

My father's arrogance and refusal to listen to others is why he is dead. I am not my father!

I was taken away from the scene of the death and protected by my saviors. While with them I also learned a great many things. Things which I have since confirmed to be true. Members of the royal line are taught that the laws that were made hundreds of years ago when this colony was founded were still being upheld. I was taught that from the time I was a hatchling. However, I was lied to. I was told that the laws of how our colony was to acquire workers were still being carried out. That was a LIE!" Yari's voice rose loudly with accusation.

"People from other worlds are being abducted by FORCE. Brought here against their will. Abused or killed all so other people can profit off their lives. That is against the laws of our colony and it has been since the start! I was raised to believe that slaves just like to complain a lot. That they are paid well enough, but they want more than they earn. I was told that they volunteer to work here and that their families are heavily compensated before they are brought here. That was a complete work of fiction! I was told that slaves are free to go after the terms of their contract are up. I found that most have no contract at all! I was also told that once a slave is brought here, none have been allowed to leave in over two hundred years. *NONE.*

Legally the contracts were meant to be for five, ten, or fifteen years, with an option for permanent residency at the end of the fifteen year contract. They would no longer be slaves after fifteen years. They would become low cast. That has not happened!

I have seen first had the horrible abuse done to those who are not sold at the auction. Their lives thrown away for no good reason. Our laws have not been kept! *THAT CHANGES NOW!*" He said with a shout.

"There is no way that I can bring back the dead. I cannot change the past, but I *CAN* see to it that our laws are upheld in the way they were written by our founders. The first order that I am issuing as Emperor is this: In repayment for the sins of my father and those like him, I am freeing all slaves! All contracts are null and void. The people were brought here against their will. That automatically voids *ANY* ownership contracts."

I could hear the cheering of the slave sections of the city all the way across the city as well as the furious shouts of many of the merchants and other casts.

Yari raised his hand, "Silence! Give me silence. There is more you must hear."

The crowds slowly calmed and he continued speaking, "Those who agree to stay and continue working will do so under legal contracts with living wages and the rights of full citizens. Those who wish to leave, may do so with back pay for the time they were held against their will. We will arrange for people to be returned to their home worlds if that is their wish. I will also allow people to bring their families here if they desire that. They are now free people and can do as they please."

"As your emperor, I hope you choose to stay and help reshape this world into what it is meant to be. I hope you will work with me to bring us into the future. Bring me your ideas on ways to improve our city, on new business, or inventions. I want to start a new wave of growth and expansion in our city that will benefit all people. Yes, there is money to be made, but it will not be at the expense of the slaves. We need to step forward. It will be scary to many, but it is worth doing! We can all have a better future if we all work together as one people and not as casts and not as owners of slaves. I am your emperor, but I am also following the laws as they are written by the founders. I am not rewriting the laws. I am enforcing them as they were intended."

The cheering from the crowds was loud enough that

the stone walls began to shake. I feared for Yari, I knew that people who try to bring changes like this often end up martyred. I feared all along that I would be one as well. I looked out over the city and saw that there were people cheering not just from the slave section, but from the tops of buildings in every circle. Even the high cast roofs were covered in people cheering and waving strips of cloth. I was not naive enough to think that there would be no resistance. But from this reaction: those that resist would be greatly outnumbered. Like my mate said, if more people opposed slavery than those who wanted it then slavery could be abolished.

I looked at my mate and saw he had his hands over his mouth. Tears were streaming down his face. This was because of him. Yari had listened to him and kept his promises to help. As Yari stepped away from the platform, he walked to my mate and embraced him before pressing their foreheads together.

"Thank you," my mate choked out.

"Do you think Abraham would be proud of me?"

"I think so," my mate laughed

When Yari stepped back I held my arms out for my mate who leaned into my chest as he wiped at his face. I looked to my parents who were still standing in shock. My brother jumped up and down shouting like only a child could. Yari turned to him and held out his arm.

Relin ran to him and jumped into his arms. He swung him around in circles before putting him down again.

Many of the fancily dressed people looked furious as Yari led us past them, however, some were smiling and more than a few shed tears. As we walked past the end of the line Yari spotted the little girl who had been the table for our lunch. He stopped before her and knelt down before her.

"You will never be treated as a piece of furniture again," he reached up and carefully unwound the ring that had been woven into her hair. He then threw the ceramic ring onto the ground and shattered it.

He turned to the shocked row behind us.

"People will be treated with respect regardless of what caste they may be. Children will not be abused like this again."

Turning to the little girl he knelt down again, "Is your family here?"

She looked confused, "I have no family."

"You are an orphan?"

"No. I was raised in the training quarters. We have no parents."

"Training quarters?"

"Yari," my mother spoke quietly. "They come and take newly hatched young from people like us. We had two sons taken, we have no idea what happened to them. It's possible that is what she means."

A look of horror and then anger crossed his face. "Garen!" He yelled loudly.

The very flustered advisor hurried forward, "Yes, Emperor Yari."

"Is it true that hatchlings are stolen from their parents?"

"I believe so." He said quietly.

"Are they sent to the training centers?"

"Yes, Emperor." He bowed his head.

"Then what? What happens to them?"

"They are trained for roles throughout the city from guards, to service people, servants and other roles."

"And they are denied knowledge of their parents?"

"Yes."

"This practice ends today. While it may be difficult to carry out, I want people to be able to find their stolen children. This practice was not in the founders laws. I will be adding a law banning the practice immediately."

"Yes, Emperor." He bowed before hurrying away again. That poor man was going to have a heart attack by the end of the day.

Yari turned back to the little girl, "You do have a family, but you just don't know them yet. In the meantime, come with me." He held out his hand and she took it smiling. He took the tray from her hand and passed it to his cousin who grinned at him and nodded.

We followed him to the royal quarters where Yari sat back on a heavily ornate couch. I had never imagined such luxury in my life.

"I will have you shown to rooms in a while. You can choose which ones you want as your own. Please feel free to change, " he paused, "everything".

"You're amazing, Yari. Don't ever let anyone tell you different," my mate said from where he sat next to me.

"Thank you, my friend. I can only hope that people take this to heart. I want more for all of my people than what they had before."

"I can still hear the celebrating of the freed slaves from here," Yari grinned. "I'm sure their former masters are extremely angry with me right now though, and ultimately most of them answer to the high caste. The high caste may have to answer to me, but they do hold a lot of power. Right now, they are likely plotting my death. For that, I need to put my own plan into play."

"What do you have in mind?"

"I need protection, from those who will be loyal to me. I have a feeling all those who were raised in the training center are likely controlled by the high caste." He looked at the little girl who sat beside him. She nodded slightly.

"That is why they took so many children to have raised as they saw fit. They wanted to have numbers that were higher than the slave numbers. What they don't know is that the slaves are about to get their children back."

There was a scratch at the closed door, my father went to answer it. He let in the advisor who led at least a dozen people who each used rolling carts to pull heavy carts of scrolls.

"I took all the records I could get. It looks like they kept records of everything. I have been told that all those raised in the training centers are marked on their wrists with numbers which correspond to these records."

"You're joking? It can't be that easy." My mate blurted out.

The advisor ignored him.

"Bring all of them and come with me." Yari walked us all the way back to the podium.

The bells tolled again and the celebrating calmed quickly. "This is for the former slaves who had children stolen from them. I have recovered scrolls which list the names of the parents and the number of the infant who was taken. That number is marked on the wrist of the ones taken. Those people were then trained to be guards and other roles around the city. Both the people who had their hatchlings stolen and those who were raised in the training center can retrieve the information by coming to the gate of the royal level. Harassment of anyone traveling along the path between the walls will not be tolerated. For my part, I am deeply sorry that your hatchlings were taken from you. It should never have happened. I hope that this helps bring you peace." Yari stepped back and walked towards us.

One guard stepped forward, "Emperor Yari, if I may..." he paused.

"You want to know if your records are in there." The tall male nodded.

"We were told that we were hatched from eggs created from donated materials, that we didn't have parents and that we are not real people because we were never laid."

Yaris jaw dropped right along with the rest of us.

He stepped closer, "You are a real person. What is your name?"

"15791." He answered quickly.

Yari blinked before looking at the girl next to him.

"23874." She said quietly. "They tell us we don't have names because we are not people."

"That is sickening. From now on you will have names. Spread the word among all of the people from the training center. Choose your own names and that is what you will be called. No one is a number anymore."

The guard fought back emotion from his eyes, "I will, my emperor." He bowed low.

"Rise and lets find the names for you."

"Yari, it looks like they are arranged by year." His

cousin said as she looked at the ends of the scrolls.

"I am twenty-two years old." The guard said.

After searching the scrolls they located three. Each was also marked with the start and finishing numbers of that scroll. Grabbing the middle scroll Yari knelt down on the courtyard   floor.

"15791 was it?" Yari asked.

"Yes, my Emporer," he said also kneeling down.

"Just call me Yari please, I prefer it."

The guard nodded quietly. "Thank you, Yari. You have no idea how much what you have done today means to all of us."

"I only want what is best for all my people." He patted that guards, arm before rolling the scrolls out. He rolled it out slowly. The sheer number of listings was sickening Looking down the list Yari finally spoke, "Here! It says Ga'Nor and Derse with the residence listed as deep tunnel 453 room slot 4."

"May I go there?"

Yari nodded, "With my blessings. You are the first to know. I realize that we have lost many in the past few days, which will likely make many reunions impossible. Spread the word that no one is without family. If they no longer have living family, they have us."

He nodded and rose, "Thank you my emperor, Yari."

He left at a jog and Yari re rolled the scroll. "Take

these down to the gates and recruit everyone you think you will need to help."

"Yes Emperor Yari, and thank you." He nodded before raising up his own sleeve. Yari stepped up to him. "You are a good man, Garen. I have always respected you. I am sure your parents are proud of you. Be sure to look up your number as well. If not, you have me."

"Yes my emperor," Garen said.

"Just call me Yari,"

"Yes, Yari, thank you."

As Garen walked away, helping to push the heavy carts, I couldn't help but smile, "Gee, you think THAT just undermined their little plan?" I had to stifle my laugh.

"Just a bit," Yari laughed.

I expected that Yari would be confronted by anger right away over his decisions, but most of the people who were not happy chose to hold their tongues for now at least. We went to the Royal estate again to settle in for a while. I was grateful for the incredible room we were given. My mate and I loved it. The furniture was not to our tastes, but the bed was incredible. We were quick to put it to good use.

CHAPTER NINE

Sean

Yari was amazing, wasn't he?" I asked as we lay resting after the long adventures we had been on.

"Yes, he is. He is right to worry about becoming a martyr, though." De'Ceer said.

"I do fear for him, but I think that even if he is killed, it will not stop what he has started. As he said, though, he was not reinventing laws, but enforcing the way they were written in the first place. That means that slavery was not legal here. Somewhere along the line," I paused. "How many people do you think will leave?"

"Some will, no doubt. But truthfully, I can see them coming back because what they knew back home is likely gone."

"I wouldn't go home. I miss my friends back home, but my family is here." I looked at him and grinned. "I am home."

He pulled me close to him and held me tightly in his arms. The infected brand on my chest had been treated and now looked much better. My forehead and cheek were still scratched up and a bit bruised from where my face had hit the ground, but it was healing well enough. I didn't know if I would have scars, but I don't think that would bother my mate.

We had taken turns making love this time. It was so amazing to feel my mate as he shuddered his way through an orgasm while riding me. He took me a short time later. His confidence in our love making had grown so much since we started. He knew how my body worked and he could turn me inside out with a few short strokes. My sweet mate had the most expressive face of any male I had ever seen. He doesn't hide his emotions, he tells people the truth, sometimes bluntly, but he does what is right. I knew he was an honorable man the day he plucked me up out of the sands and saved me from the storm. I held him close, his cool skin warming where our bodies touched, he moaned and moved closer to me.

"I love how you warm me. Your seed warms me from the inside in a way I never imagined possible."

We were considering another round when we heard a frantic scratching at the door. We jumped from the bed and quickly dressed. Throwing the door open, my father waved us out to the corridor.

"You need to come quickly, you won't believe this."

We hurried after my father who was also coaxing along Relin, who was groggily waking up.

We reached the entry room where Yari stood with two guards.

I watched as De'Ceer's father got his mother. She was still blinking her eyes sleepily. I can see where Relin gets his morning issues from. She stumbled, half-awake after her mate.

"My love," he turned to his mate, "we found them."

"What?" She said, blinking her eyes?

"Our boys," he started to laugh and cry at the same time before pointing to the two guards standing next to Yari. Yari had his hand over his mouth watching.

My jaw dropped. Those two guards were their sons, De'Ceer's older brothers. I looked at him and he stood, completely still, just staring at them. I looked at the two men. I could see a very strong family resemblance, De'Ceer was the spitting image of his eldest brother where as Rilen looked more like the other brother. The guards didn't seem to know what they were supposed to do as their mother launched at them, sobbing. They still wore their heavy armor and weapons. The two men held still while their parents went back and forth between them.

I could tell they were totally overwhelmed and had

shut down. Walking over I whispered to De'Ceer's father that the males were overwhelmed and needed a moment.

He agreed and helped his wife to the seating area. Relin had stayed back, well away from the situation. He looked confused and maybe a little frightened of them.

I led the males into one of the vacated rooms and told them to take their armor off. They looked nervous about it.

"It's scaring your little brother."

"We have a little brother?" the taller one asked.

"You have two, my mate is De'Ceer, the elder of your two brothers. Relin is the other. He's still a child and he's afraid of the armor and weapons."

"We are not permitted to remove them outside of our sleep chamber. We already broke the rules by removing our helmets.

"You are safe. No one is going to get mad at you. Come and join your family. They have missed both of you terribly."

"We didn't know we had parents. We didn't know we were even brothers, though we did know we looked similar."

"You have each other, but you also have us. Come join us." I nodded.

They slowly began removing their armor. I realized with a shock that the armor didn't just attach to its self, but to them. They had bolts drilled into their bones that held the armor in place. They had sections where the armor looked to have warn the skin away so many times they scarred.

Finally, the two men stood wearing only their under loin cloths. I found some simple tunics for them to wear and a pair of simple pants. They had difficulty getting into the clothing. They had never worn anything like it before. My heart broke for them. I helped them get ready and brought them back out again.

"Relin, come and meet your brothers." I told him gently.

He looked at them nervously, "Are you really my brothers?"

They both nodded. The tall one spoke, "We did not know we had brothers, or parents."

"I don't know what I am supposed to do." The other said quietly.

I walked up behind him and motioned for him to move closer to Relin. Finally the tall one knelt down. "I do not know how to be an older brother. Will you teach me?"

Relin nodded and put his arms around his brother's neck. I could see him tense as if expecting to be strangled, but he blinked slowly and his head came down to rest on top of his brothers.

"My brother," he said softly. Moments later all four

males were embracing while their parents looked on happily. I walked to Yari, "Did you have something to do with this?"

"Maybe a little. I also had them transferred here to my personal guard. I will assign them to guard their family. That way they don't have to leave at all."

I leaned into him, "Abraham would be proud."

"I hope so". He reached up and began to rub his fingers on a familiar small coin that had been placed as the center of an amulet that now hung around his neck. I stifled a laugh. Americans would think that was a bit laughable, but I think Yari will wear that as emperor. Frankly, it suited him rather nicely.

CHAPTER TEN

De'Ceer

I was rather overwhelmed by the frantic pace of Yari's changes, as I am sure everyone in our world was. My deep concern for his safety as well as our own was proved warranted only hours after we had retired for the night. I lay with my mate in our heated sleeping pallet when I heard a loud explosion. I vaulted out of bed, grabbed my startled mate, and ran from our room. I could scent smoke as it began to flood down our hallway. My family, including my older brothers, all scurried out of our room and away from the smoke. If not for their quick thinking, we may all have been killed. No sooner had they secured us inside a hidden passageway than an even greater explosion rocked the thick walls around us. We were hurried downward to a small chamber which Yari, his cousin, and a number of other people were now secured. He hurried to us and made certain that we were all accounted for and none were injured.

"They think that they succeeded in killing me. Yari laughed. They only succeeded in blowing up a mock figure of me lying in my bed. Fools. I should have anticipated that they would also attack all of you, for that I am very sorry. That is a mistake that will not happen again. It would seem that some of the guards are still loyal to the high caste. They are the ones who carried out this attack. However, they have already been taken into custody and, with luck, we will soon know who sent them."

"Yari, I cannot allow my children to stay here. It is simply too dangerous."

"It is also far too dangerous for you to leave as well. I do have a plan, if you will give me time to make the arrangements."

My father nodded, I could see the worry in his eyes.

Yari nodded as well as he stepped away to speak with my brothers. They both snapped to attention and nodded before they turned on their heels and left. I knew my mother would become very upset by their leaving, so I wrapped my arms around her and held her.

"They will return." I told her quietly. My father came and took her into his arms. My little brother clung to my mate. His eyes still wide with terror. His tail wrapped tightly around my mate's thigh. Sean's eyes shone with fear as much as my brothers. I went to him and kissed his lips. My own parents' lips quirked up. Apparently they had discovered that they liked the mouth mating as well. My mother said it was so unique and beautiful.

We settled down on the heating rocks in the corner of the room and waited nervously for the return of our brothers. There was another massive explosion and my mother screamed, and tried to run up the stairs after my brothers. Thankfully, they emerged moments later and motioned for us to follow them.

Yari helped to guide his cousin down the narrow stairway. We went down into an area which was so cold my bones ached and every step became painful. Sean clutched my brother to his chest and wrapped his cloak around him tightly. I knew that Sean's body heat would keep my brother from feeling the pain of this walk. We went down another flight of stairs before I scented water ahead. More water than I had ever scented in my life.

We emerged from the tunnel to see a massive body of water. I heard Yari cursing. He held up a broken rope, "The water floating vessel broke loose!"

"There it is." My eldest brother pointed. It sat against the rocks on the other side of the water. "We cannot reach it. We are trapped."

"Is there anything in that water that could be

dangerous? Carnivorous creatures? Deadly parasites?" Sean asked.

"No, the water is pure. But it is very cold."

Sean reached down and put his hand in the water, "It's cool, but not as cold as the water I grew up swimming in all the time."

"That word does not translate."

"Moving about in the water. I will swim over and get the boat. I just wanted to make sure there was nothing in there that would attack me."

"There is nothing. This is a contained water supply that our founders started to take care of our people, it is rationed out, but we add to it from the spires above." Yari pointed to the tubes from above that dripped slowly into the dark water below.

My mate passed my brother to me and wrapped his still warm cloak around us. He quickly shed all of his clothing and I began to grow more and more concerned.

"Sean, that water is far above your head!" Yari warned.

"It's okay. I was born in water." Sean went to the edge and walked out into the water and felt for the edge. When he found it, he stepped out and disappeared under the water. I screeched in terror and tried to charge forward. My family held me back as I continued to screech and tried to reach for him. I watched as Sean's head emerged over the surface and he waved. He began making strange motions with his arms and kicking his legs as he moved quickly through the water. He crossed the water like one of the sand quirns digs through the dunes, his body moving with ease and grace. He dipped below the surface as he neared the boat. He came up fast, grabbing the edge of the water floating vessel, and he pulled himself up and out of the water. He flipped inside and looked around. I could hear him laughing and he put two long sticks into posts on the sides and then pushed away from the rocks. With a lunge forward, he dipped the long sticks into the water and as he pulled back on the sticks the vessel moved quickly forward. He guided it with skill and ease. He angled it sideways against the rocks and motioned for us to climb down into it.

"It's a row boat! Just like the ones I grew up with. Keep your bodies low, stay in the center and I will direct you were to sit to keep the weight evenly distributed. We don't want to flip the boat over. Do *NOT* lean over the edges. Just stay where I put you."

We all nodded in agreement. Tipping over would kill all of us, except my mate apparently. Born in water? I had never heard of such a thing, it was nearly sacrilegious! He directed one of my brothers to the front and one to the back to balance out their heavy weights. Then, he had my father go to the back, my mother and brother to the front and he had me sit on the seat just behind him. He directed Yari's cousin to sit next to my mother. Last was Yari who held the row boat steady. He put him on the row just in front of him. The row boat rocked ominously as Sean pushed it away from the rocks. He used the big sticks to guide us were Yari directed us to go. We had to pass through a very long, extremely dark passage for a long distance. My mate started to rub his hands and laugh, saying that his calluses from rowing when he was a kid had softened so his hands would have blisters from this. He also mentioned that he would be sore from using muscles that were unused to this work.

"How do you know to do this? You really had access to this much water when you were a child?" Yari asked him.

"More than seventy percent of my planet is covered in water. Even the land has large bodies of water. My parents' house was on a lake. That's fresh water, the oceans are salt water. I spent every day when the weather was good, swimming, fishing, or out on my boat. I miss it actually. I lived on the coast of one of the massive saltwater oceans on my world. I would swim sometimes, but the water is much colder and the rip tides can be very dangerous. There are also things in the oceans that would just love to eat us, like sharks. It doesn't happen often, but it does happen."

"That's impossible!" Yari gasped. "How can so much of your world be covered in water?"

Sean shrugged, "How come yours isn't? I think my home world must be very, very far from here. We have one sun, one moon, and a huge amount of water. We do still have massive deserts, shockingly high mountains, vast plains, the ice caps on the poles, and our climate ranges from extremely hot to extremely cold, very wet, to very, very dry."

"What are Ice poles?" Yari asked.

"We call the Northern most point of our world the north pole, and the southernmost point the south pole. They are both covered in ice. That's frozen water."

"What does frozen mean?" My mother asked. "That word does not translate."

"When water reaches a very low temperature, it becomes a solid mass. Water that is at a moderate temperature is a liquid and water, which is heated above the boiling point, becomes a gas."

"That I knew." My mother said, "But a solid? You mean like sand?"

"Sort of. It can be. If you were to take a cup of water and put it into a freezer it would become completely hard like a stone. If you tipped the cup out onto a table it would not spill. It would thunk onto the table like a rock. It would be hard as one, practically. But as the temperature comes out, it would slowly melt and return back to its liquid state."

I looked at Yari and his eyes were wide in shock.

"And you have seen this?"

"We use ice all the time. We put it in our drinks to make them cold. When the temperature outside drops below freezing and it rains, what comes down is frozen water that we call snow. That snow can accumulate in large amounts and last for a long time. Up at the high altitudes on mountains, we love to go skiing. That's sliding down huge slopes of snow and ice with long flat boards on our feet. OH! I have a picture of me as a kid skiing actually. Take my wallet out of my back pocket."

I reached into his clothing and pulled out his folded leather item keeper. He told me to open it up and there are pictures inside. I began to look through them, some were ruined from the water, but I saw one of Sean as a young male, in a fluffy strange looking garment of bright colors, he wore a brightly colored hat, and held two sticks in his hands, and wore one board on each foot. He stood on white sand and all around him was white. I saw tall shaped things all around him that I did not understand that also had more white sand on them. All around him I could see people sliding down the hill on the boards. I showed it to my family and they gasped in shock. Yari examined it carefully before handing it back. I looked at the picture of him and his family. That was when I realized what was behind them. A huge body of water. I had thought it was a stone. I gasped at the massive amount of water. I passed that to Yari and his hands shook as he held the picture.

"You speak the truth!"

Sean simply nodded and kept pulling on the sticks.

I looked through the pictures, there were not many that had gone undamaged, but I saw one of Sean and two other males and one... female? I held that one up.

"Those are my friends Dave and Manik. I was at an award party for my work with them the night I was taken. They invited me to their house for an after party. But I had to catch a flight to London the next morning. So I went home. I took a taxi, but I made the driver let me out early. He was a very unsafe driver. Nearly got us into multiple accidents. I thought I would be safer walking. I was wrong. Surprisingly, I don't regret it now, though." He looked over his shoulder and smiled at me.

"Who is this?" I pointed to the one I wasn't sure if they were male or not.

"That's Tristian. He's been my friend since I got into.. My job. He's so beautiful, it's not even believable. He really is stunning. He is also surprisingly shy and quiet too. He is amazing to work with."

"What do you do?" Yari asked.

My mate froze, then started rowing again, he sputtered slightly.

"He makes pornographic vids." My mother leaned around me to say.

"Ah... yeah," My mate seemed very uncomfortable with discussing it.

"Really?" Yari asked. "They are quite popular here."

"Ah, they are back home too... well with some people at least. Other people treat those the industry very badly. Some people from my society are extremely prudish."

"There are those here too. But it is not looked down upon here. They provide a service and many find it very stimulating if they do not have one to copulate with. It is not something we are ashamed of." My mother said simply. "The brothels are also typically considered high standards of living, and they provide for their workers well. Most of them anyway."

"There are very few places in my society where brothels are legal and most are looked down on very badly. Most people in that end of the profession are breaking the law and could be imprisoned for it, or fined. They also risk getting terrible diseases and such. I don't take risks like that. The company I work for very closely screens people they hire and test us all for diseases constantly. Before every shoot we have to pass screening. If you test positive, and it isn't something that's treatable, you're out of work. Even if you are treatable, usually your reputation is toast."

"I can understand that. We do screen here as well. We have inoculations against most diseases, but some things we can still get. Like parasites." Yari nodded, then shuddered.

"Yes, parasites can be very bad. We have to worry about them getting under our armor and into our fasteners. Those are horrific." One of my brothers said.

"God that sounds horrible." My mate gasped. "Yari, are you aware that they do not wear their armor? That armor is bolted into their bones themselves?"

I heard Yari gasp and he turned to look at my brother who sat behind him who simply nodded. He reached to his arm and removed the armor on his arms. The posts pulled out of his skin and showed the drilled in connections they attached to. Yari looked back at my mate with horror on his face.

"Is this done to all of you?"

"Yes. Some do not survive the instillation of the fasteners. There are almost five hundred in all. Other succumb to infections or parasites later. Or shattered bones. They do not bother letting us heal. They simply dispose of us."

Yari looked sickened to the point of being physically ill. "What you have suffered through, it ends now. No one else would go through such tortures."

"The high caste will not let these changes happen, not

easily." My father pointed out.

"They are about to find their power removed." Yari chuckled menacingly.

"What are you going to do?" Sean asked.

"You will see shortly. We are almost there."

My mate rowed, though I could tell his body was paining him and his hands must be hurting because he wrapped his garments around his hands to shield them from the sticks.

My mate was told to slow the rowboats forward momentum. We glided slowly toward a light source. I turned to see an opening a head. There was a flat platform and stairs led up to the light. Sean put the rowboat up to the platform and he secured it and helped us out in a specific order. The rowboat rocked ominously as my brothers climbed out. They both visibly relaxed once they were out of the rowboat. My mate pulled the boat over to a ring that was drilled into the rock and he took the rope from the front of the boat and tied it to the ring on the platform with a skillfully made knot.

He dressed in his garments again, now that he was free of water. I could see how tired he was in his every movement. He looked up at the long length of stairs and I heard him sigh before walking slowly toward them. I stopped him before he reached the stairs.

"Mate, you are too tired. Let me carry you. Get on my

back."

"De'Ceer, I can't you're..." His eyes dropped to my abdomen.

I growled, "I am stronger than you even now. Get on." I told him firmly.

He complied, but I could see he was nervous about it. I carried him with ease. He really was not very heavy. Once he seemed to realize that I was stronger than he had thought, I felt his body relax. I felt his breathing slow and was surprised when he fell asleep. I had forgotten how much more sleep his species requires than mine.

"He is exhausted." I spoke to Yari. "His species requires both much more sleep, and more water than ours."

"He will have both soon. We are nearly there." He led us up to a rocky outcropping and I saw a thick, solid panel of clear glass, into which was built a very sturdy door. Yari pressed a code into the door and it opened. He led us through it into a strange cavern of sorts. I looked around and was completely astonished by what I saw. I could not understand anything around me.

My mate stirred and woke. He looked around and gasped. He slid down from my back and began to point to different things. He knew what these things were, or at least somewhat knew.

"How do you have any of these things here? Many of

these plants have been extinct, or at least mostly so, for millions of years on my world."

"Most of these were brought back from seeds found in the drifting sands. Some of the animals were brought here from other planets in our galaxy." Yari told him. "This place was constructed by our founders. This was to be their gift for the future. This place was nearly lost. The people who were entrusted in its care protect this place, and it became a very closely guarded secret. So much so, that for many generations, they cut themselves off from our society because they did not trust that we would keep this place pure.

I found this place by accident in my youth. I crossed the waters in the rowboat and came here. I got through the door by trying random numbers, and then ones that I guessed might have had significance. The number that finally worked should have been obvious, but it wasn't. The people who guard this place, are shy, but I think they will interest your mate."

Sean's brows furrowed as the strange things behind Yari parted. My mate gasped, the one the stepped through looked similar to him, they were different colors, but of similar type.

"You're human!" My mate nearly shouted.

Yari spoke words to the male and he looked over Sean with curiosity. He came to him and began to poke at his skin. Apparently he had not seen one like him before.

"How do you have humans here?"

"The founders rescued them from slavers as they were constructing this place. Their numbers have grown to nearly two thousand. I have made sure that they are all inoculated so they will not be vulnerable to diseases or health issues. They are the caretakers of this sacred place, I became the caretaker of the caretakers. I guessed you were the same species, despite your differing appearance."

"Yes, we are the same species. They are descended from another content on my world than my ancestors came from. Where their ancestors were from has harsher, brighter light and much higher temperatures, my ancestors were from a cold climate that was more wet and did not require as much protection from the sun."

"Ah! I see. Regional adaptations. That is a common occurrence in a wide variety of species." Yari nodded. "This is Ruik. I have known him since I was young. He understands what we say because I gave him an implant. Not many of the others have the implants. He will help speak for you if you need it."

The male nodded.

"I didn't think I would see another human again." My mate said. I could see his happiness at seeing another of his kind. The male reached out and put his arm around him. He gave him a firm pat on the back. I felt a sudden surge of jealousy and I began to snarl before I could stop myself. The male instantly drew a very sharp looking knife on the end of a long thin shaft.

Yari spoke with him quickly and he lowered his weapon. He said something to Yari who sighed.

"He meant no offence. He did not see that your mate was marked. His people mark their mates in a different way. He apologizes."

"He understands us?"

Yari nodded.

"Then can you talk to us?"

The male paused, "Yes, bright skin."

My mate smiled, "My name is Sean."

"You are not diseased to be so light?" He asked.

My mate shook his head, "Where I am from there are people with many colors of skin, hair, and eyes. Many heights, many weights, many body types."

"I am Ruik. Most are like me." He turned and walked through the strange things I had no words for.

"Ruik? Are there dangerous things like spiders or snakes here?"

"Yes. Walk where I walk. Only."

He led the way through the path I was amazed. Everywhere I looked was something knew and indescribable.

CHAPTER ELEVEN

Sean

I never thought I would be walking through a prehistoric jungle, led by a guy that looked like he was right out of a drawing of ancient Africans. His clothes were fascinating. He was beautiful in a way that I found alluring. I wasn't turned on by him like I was for De'Ceer, but I could see myself going for him if I was not with De'Ceer.

The jungle around us was extremely primitive. The air was hot and humid. Then it dawned on me:

"Yari, how do you keep this place a secret? Wouldn't anyone who sees this place from above find it?"

"We use technology to hide it. We disguise it so it looks like just another sand drift. You will see more, soon."

We were led to a rocky ledge and looked down over a valley which looking like nothing I could ever have imagined. "It's like stepping back in time!"

"I am not certain why this looks like your world did long ago. But I know that this world was not always as dry as it is now. Something happened to make it lose most of its moisture. That is what we are going to change." Yari smiled at me.

"What?" I asked confused.

"The founders never intended our world to be a nearly unlivable desert, it did not start off that way. Someone stopped the process that would have made it more livable. The high caste are the ones the control the water. By controlling the water, they control the people. That is how they will quell any rebellion. They shut off all water, and people submit, or die. I am going to restart the process that the founders started."

"It is time?" Ruik asked.

"Yes, my friend. I am emperor now. It is time."

Ruik grinned wide, his pearly white teeth showing brightly. "I will spread your order, Bringer of the Water."

Yari nodded and Ruik took off at a run down the path. I watched him easily sprint down a path that I would have broken my damned ankle on at a walk. Hell, if I tried to run on it, I would have gotten down into the valley the fast way. That would have been the end of me!

I heard a loud horn sounding and then more horns echoed all across the valley. As more and more horns sounded, creatures flew up into the air, startled. I looked around as a strange rumbling sounded under our feet.

"What is that?"

"They reactivated the machines that will bring water to this world. They not only tend to this place, but they tend to the machines that are spread out all over this planet, hidden from view. You will see the change in as little as a day." Yari's smile slowly spread over his face. "Come with me, my friends."

He walked with us slowly down a long steady decline to a hollow within the rocks. There was an entire city carved out of the stone hillside. They used natural materials to construct the most incredible city I had ever seen. Living plants were twisted and manipulated into bridges, into railings, and I saw people come out from the buildings to gape at me and the others. Relin looked downright afraid of them. I reached out and took his hand. He looked at me nervously as we walked behind Yari.

I yawned, feeling so tired that even this incredible place could not keep me awake any longer. Thankfully Yari led us up a vine stairway to a large open area on a higher level. He took us across the open expanse and greeted an elderly man and woman with outstretched arms. They embraced and he introduced them to us as the leaders of their people. They greeted us each in turn before we were led to a place where would could rest.

I did not want to sleep, but by then, I was too tired not to. I lay down on the thick pad of woven fibers that rested on top of a thick bed of what looked like giant leaves that had been layered hundreds thick before being having the woven mat placed over them. I lay down, and even though it was not what I would consider comfortable. De'Ceer's strong arms held me from behind. His tail wrapped up and over my legs and came to rest under my head. My arms wrapped around his tail. I loved the feeling of his steading breathing across my neck. I knew he was now gravid. I was still trying to wrap my mind around that concept. I also knew that he was not particularly happy about it. Actually he was still pretty pissed off to be honest. I wasn't unaware of that fact. I had no idea what our offspring would look like, but I was so eager to find out. I pushed back against his body and he tightened his arms around me. I yawned and was asleep moments later.

I awoke sometime much later to a cool bed and no De'Ceer. I knew that I require far more sleep than he does, but it would be nice to wake up with him for once. I got up, stretched and went to look for him. I found Ruik on the walkway near where we had slept.

"How are you?" I asked.

"Confused." He stated plainly.

"About what?"

"You."

"Me?"

"Yes. You claim to be my species. But you do not look like me."

"Ah, yes. We have different colors, but we are both human."

"But you share you bed with one of them?"

"He is my mate."

I saw Ruik's jaw twitch.

"I take it that you do not approve?" I crossed my arms over my chest."

"You and I are not the same. But you claim we are the same species."

"Ah. Now I see." I turned to walk away from him. I heard him snarl and I turned just in time to see his speer lash through the air. I twisted and ducked. I rolled, went over the edge of the ledge and nearly missed grabbing the bottom of the vine walkway bellow it. I swung into the space. People gasped and jumped to their feet. Ruik dropped in front of me, his spear still out. He tried to shove it at me again but I dove to the side again, I took off at a run. I knew I couldn't out run him. I couldn't dive out of the way forever. That one was going to kill me, and likely his friends would too. I ran for the vines that led back to my level and I saw Ruik hurl the spear at me. It never reached me.

De'Ceer smacked it out of the way with his tail as he launched his body between us. From the edge of the walkway.

"*YOU DARE ATTACK MY MATE!*" He roared so loudly his voice echoed down the valley. I heard other bellowing roars answer his. I knew his family was on their way.

"What is the meaning of this!" Yari walked up behind Ruik.

"He attacked me! He is a spy!"

"Attacked *YOU*? You're the one that was waiting for me to wake. You confronted me about your belief that I'm not *REALLY* your species because I am a different color... and how much you disapprove that my mate is not my own species. *THEN*, you attacked me!'

"You are *NOT* my species!" Ruik sneered.

"Really?" I reached into my wallet, thumbed through my pictures and held up the picture of me with my friends. "Really? You see this? We are all different colors."

The leader of his people came up, and took the picture. He looked at it then nodded. "He speaks true." Then he translated it for those who could not understand. "Ruik, you have made a very serious accusation. What proof do you have that he is a spy?'

"This." He held up a small disk. I looked at it.

"I have no idea what that is. I have never seen

anything like it."

"That is a tracking device." One of De'Ceer's brothers grabbed it and smashed it. "Where did you find this?"

"Near his sleeping pad." Ruik snarled.

"First, why were you near his sleeping pad while he slept?" Yari spoke. His voice low and cold.

"I protect my people."

"And that could not have been on him. I would have seen it. I would have felt it in his clothing. He took everything off to swim to reach the boat. So, tell me, Ruik, where do you propose he hid it?"

He paused a moment too long.

"That was not placed by Sean. Ruik. We have been friends our entire lives. Why are you doing this?"

"I do nothing. You should know me better that that."

"Until this moment, I would have said that I did. You attack someone I call a friend. Someone I owe a life debt to. You use that as proof? Why would he smuggle that here to someplace he did not know he was going, to a people he never knew existed, and then leave it lying on the ground in open view? Ruik. There is no logic in that."

"This place is sacred. They should not be here."

"So you used that to summon people who would destroy this place?"

Ruik spun to face Yari. "I would never do that!"

"That is what that device does. It summons the guards

that no doubt still follow us, bent on killing us. My friend. Think with reason."

"I did not place it there."

"Then who did?"

"My people do not leave this place." Ruik said quickly.

I looked around at each of the faces I had come to care about I paused on his De'Ceers brothers. They both stared ahead too stiffly.

"Yari, I think I know who did it." I said quietly.

Yari's gaze followed mine.

"Please tell me that this is not so? Which of you has done this. Which of you led those who would kill your family right here?"

Neither of them spoke.

Their mother walked up to them, "You truly do not believe that we are your family, do you? Remove your masks."

Neither complied.

Yari walked slowly around them and they did not move. His hands darted up and touched a place on both of their necks. They both crumped to the ground while their family shriek in fear.

"Remove their armor. All of it. Inspect it for more tracking devices. Then dispose of their armor. Ruik, I will need tools and awakening potions." Ruik turned to leave, "Ruik."

He paused and looked back over his shoulder.

"Do not let your own prejudices keep you from seeing the truth."

Ruik nodded then hurried away.

I worked to remove the armor. It was more difficult than I had anticipated. With help, both brothers were freed from their armor. Each of them had several more tracking devices as well as an assortment of other rather scary looking things hidden away under their armor.

"I'm just guessing, but that's poison isn't it?" I pointed to the small pile of vials on the ground."

"Yes. I suspect that it is." He nodded with a frustrated sigh.

It took time but Ruik returned with a bucket of what looked like crushed leaves and berries in steaming water.

He scooped out a small wooden cup's worth and held up first one brother, then the other. Each was forced to take down the liquid one cup at a time until they began to groan and their heads tossed.

"The paralytic is wearing off, now they will receive their awakening. While they are still asleep, we need to remove all of this metal from them."

The process took a team of people on each man, working throughout the day and the following night. Blood seeped from their bodies and they both moaned in pain. When the moaning got too intense, they were given more of the liquid. After we ran our hands over their entire bodies from scalp to toes and were positive that we had removed all of the ports, they were each given slow sips of another liquid. A mouthful every few minutes until their bleeding slowed and their blood was able to finally clot.

"They will suffer through much pain in the days to come, but they will heal. Rather, they will heal physically, but I cannot speak for mentally. They have both been heavily brainwashed. It may take years for them to face reality with a clear mind." Ruik sighed. His gaze looked back and forth between the brothers. "What was done to them is a hideous abuse of your people, Yari. What do you intend to do about it?"

"I have already begun to address it, but I have no doubt that those who work against me are regaining control right now. I must go back to the capital city."

"You will not go alone." De'Ceer bowed his head. His family all bowed their heads as well. I stepped up next to them. I put my closed fist over my heart. I was surprised when they all mimicked my motion.

I watched out of the corner of my eye as people along the walkway repeated the motion. I had a feeling that the motion was about to become their equivalent of a salute. I knew that this was a turning point in what would likely become a civil war. I cringed to think how many of the people around me (including myself) could die for our loyalty.

"We must return to the city, but first, we must plan quickly or all will be lost before we have even begun." De'Ceer said, his brow ridges drawn down.

"We already have the support of the slaves, we also need the support of the merchant class; what would win them over?" I asked.

"Money. If we made it financially viable for them to turn on the high caste that would bring more to my side," Yari said, rubbing his fingers along his jaw line. "Ruik, do your people still mine the crystals in the deep passages for energy?"

A smile spread over his face, "We have entire caverns filled with them."

"Crystals?" I asked.

Ruik went to one of the small lamps on the wall that I had assumed were filled with oil or the like. He pulled it down, opened the chamber, and reveled a tiny chip of crystal that glowed with incredible brightness and heat as well. "We simply expose them to the sun during the day and they can glow and emit heat all night. This small chip is enough to light an average bed area and to keep a person warm during the colder nights."

I looked at Yari, "I believe I see what you mean. This would been an incredibly popular item for people both on this world, and off world as well. Hell, even on my world they would want to get their hands on these! They would pay a fortune for them."

"Then we have our means of winning over the merchant class." Ruik nodded. "We will bring some of these to show them, but we will keep the supply low enough that the value will be kept high."

"Can these be weaponized?" I asked. They looked at me in confusion.

"May I see that?" I asked.

Ruik handed over the canister, he warned that the crystals can become very hot in the light. I used several small metal wires that I bent around the crystal to form a cage around that would protect my hand. I took it to a sunny area, then moved it around slowly until I bought it to focus on a single point. I anchored it into that place and watched in shock as not only did it form a beam of light, but the intensity of it equaled that of a high powered laser. I grabbed a piece of leather and it sliced through it with ease. I covered the sunlight going in and the beam continued for a few seconds. It could store the energy briefly. The crystal glowed so brightly now that I couldn't look at it directly. I tipped it back into the canister and sealed it, it glowed brightly, and the heat was like a furnace.

I picked up the burned leather and held it up, "This

could be a weapon if harnessed properly. That means that these could also be used against us."

Ruik took the leather and looked at it carefully. "How did you know how to do that?"

"We use focused light on my world for many purposes, including as lasers to cut things."

"Perhaps we need to rethink the crystals, if my mate was so easily able to make a weapon from it?" De'Ceer nodded slowly.

"Perhaps you are right. The last thing we need is to give them a weapon which has the potential to harm us." Yari nodded. "What else can be used to win over the merchant   class?"
"Seeing as how none of your people had thought to domesticate the local wildlife before your father, I highly doubt that you had things like horse carts or wagons to transport people or supplies?"

"Your words do not translate." De'Ceer told me. I grinned and sat down to draw out what wagons, simple horse carts, and other pulled vehicles looked like, pack animal saddles for mule trains were like, etcetera. As I described the fancy wagons and chariots that had been used on earth in ancient times Yari moved closer, his interest peaked.

"That would be exceedingly popular here, even if we do not domesticate more wildlife. That would speed production and transport goods without having to pay off worlders to use their ships to fly from one settlement to the next, only the high caste have shuttles."

"I can see a huge market for cart dealers here." I chuckled, "And for those who can breed, tame, and train the wild life here."

There were eager nods all around.

"My people can bring in more of the beasts. They come here for water frequently. We capture young or raid nests to raise them for meat. The ones we have become very tame. We have been breeding them for generations now." Ruik grinned. "Though I had not thought to put them to pull carts!"

"Or ride them." Yari grinned and Ruik's eyes went wide.

I had a feeling his people would be very busy in the next few days.

CHAPTER TWELVE

De'Ceer

My mate's intellect never ceases to amaze me. His people must truly be advanced to have such knowledge be so easily accessed by so many. I doubted that my mate was the only one from his world with such knowledge. I was eager to free more of his people, I knew that they would be an asset to us in the coming days.

Yari spread the word that we were to bring in as many beasts for training as possible. Though my mate claimed to be no expert in training of beasts, he knew exactly how to train them quickly and effectively. By trapping them in a narrow chute along a wall we were able to cover their eyes, put packs on their backs to simulate rider. They were then turned loose and lead around a large enclosed ring with high sides. We could escape under the bottom if we needed too, but the majority of the beasts quickly accepted the training, so long as their eyes were covered.

Within less than three days, we had more than a hundred beasts trained to be ridden. Even my mate was shocked by how fast the process had been. We packed our gear, some of the crystals and headed across the open desert, laden with supplies and with reinforcements. My mate was right: The predators stayed away from us so long as we had the crystals glowing brightly in the night. We made remarkable time and reached the city in only two night's travels. We stayed out of the heat in the caverns that the beasts found for us along the way.

We sheltered in my father's cave deep within the mine so that we could make our last preparations. My father and I made our way back up through the mine, only to find that many people were now taking refuge with their entire families in the deep. We instructed them to head for the opening behind us. Many were in cold shock when we found them. The high caste had ordered their troops to kill anyone that tried to stop them from taking over and reclaiming control. However, many of the guards and troops, now reunited with their families, refused to follow those orders.

We told them of the tracking devices and many went to work on removing their built in armor with the help of Ruik's people. The crystals we had brought with us saved thousands of lives by allowing people to stay in the deepest reaches without having to return to the surface for heat. We set our plan in motion slowly at first, but it caught like a fire on a dry grass mat. Within less than a week, our plans were finalized.

To win over the merchant caste, we had let them have a few crystals, only the smallest fragments, as well as giving them the plans for the carts. Within a day, they were buying up supplies to make them and setting up facilities for the beasts. The high caste paid no attention to what was going on right beneath their noses. With the help of the merchant caste, we also gained the biggest advantage we had yet: they had the purchasing power to buy out the slave houses to '*restock*' after the massive losses in the slave shelters. Rather than putting the new slaves to work in their own businesses, we paid them to send them all directly into the deep mines. We paid them handsomely for all of the slaves they purchased.

These slaves were then promptly freed, and given a choice: fight to remain free, or not fight and we would all either be killed or be returned to slavery. Hardly a one refused to fight. On the day of our planned attack, Yari and his highest ranked people returned to the palace to take his place. We sent as many of the former slaves that would be familiar with the lay out of the palace as possible in to assist them.

Yari's plan was simple: have the people who would be

least suspected place powerful sleeping drugs into all of the water which would be served to the high caste people. After some debate it was also put into the training center water supply as well because we had no idea how many of their forces would still be loyal to the high caste. I waited impatiently with my mate for word of the first stage of Yari's plan.

By midday a runner came to the deep to tell us that more than half of the high caste were captured within the first few hours. Nearly all of the rest were already detained. While there had been some fighting, there had been very little bloodshed as our forces had done their jobs very well. The high caste were now secured within the former slave quarters, locked into their domiciles. The irony did not escape me. Unlike the suffering we went through in the cold and damp: the high caste would have the benefit of the crystals which now hung in the doorway of each of their rooms, secured with heavy bolts which could only be unlocked by the guards who now held them.

Yari reclaimed his throne and ordered our people to secure his territory. We did not expect the attack to come not from his high caste people, but from above. Yari was in his command room when the palace was struck by a massive weapon blast that nearly tore the throne room in two. Blessedly, none of our people had been in the room at the time. Yari and his guards escaped into the underground, along with the majority of his supporters. Those who could not make it to the tunnels, fled the palace on foot above ground. The palace continued to be hit by weapons blasts until there was nothing left but rubble.

Seeing what was coming, Yari ordered the evacuation of the mine to the deepest reaches and for our people to withdraw from holding the high caste in the slave quarters.

We were horrified when word reached us that the slave quarters had taken direct weapons fire, again and again until every last complex had been destroyed. The majority of the high caste were killed in the attack. This was not our plan. We had not intended for them to be slaughtered where they lay confined. Yari sent a message out, in hopes of getting a reply that would tell us who was attacking us and why.

The reply was simple: They were quelling the fighting to insure that their supply from the mines returned to normal. All they cared about was their demand of minerals. Yari looked very upset, but he ordered my father to evacuate the mine. He wanted it searched so that none would be left behind. He then ordered a few of the miners to put explosives on the upper levels of the mine. One they were all cleared, the explosives were detonated, causing the upper portions of the mine to cave in. The addition of some of Ruik's crystals made the blast appear much more impressive from above. It also likely increased the overall size of the blast, but thankfully most of the blast went upwards. Truthfully, miners knew what they were doing when it came to explosives and they made it look as if the mine had completely caved in. However only the top four levels and some of the surrounding hillsides were brought down in the blast. We watched from a small outcropping of rock as the ships, which usually filled the night sky left orbit. Our concern was that they would be back for the minerals with new slave labor.

"I do not personally think they will be back," Yari said with a grunt. "For years the minerals were becoming harder and harder to reach. Many of the mines were closed now. They would likely not consider it a good investment to reopen the mine. That meant that they would no longer be interested in this world. They left behind all of the ships and shuttles which were on the planet. We scrambled to move everything to secure locations to protect them from scavengers which would come to pick at the remains of what they would assume was a dying world. The only large unnatural object in orbit was the space station, which now moved through space under minimal power.

Yari sent up troops to seize control of the station and they soon reported back that the command personal left, but there were thousands of slaves in stasis, a very large percentage of which appeared to be my mate's species. After some discussion, I agreed to go with my mate up to the station to inspect the slaves before they were brought to the planet to be awoken. The station was then staffed by Yari's people and the merchant caste readily snatched up as many store fronts and merchandise as they could grab. Within days the station was back up and running again. They broadcast that they would beat the prices of anyone in the sector for ship repairs and upgrades as well as offering refueling and other bonuses. It did not take long before the station was once again buzzing with activity. Now, the people could buy minerals directly from the miners. Which meant that the miners were able to receive much more money for their work, and buyers were paying a fraction of what they had paid the company.

Yari and his supporters had a difficult task of rebuilding the city, thanks to the devastating blasts from the attacking ships. Ultimately, it was decided that they would not rebuild the city where it had been. Instead, the entire population would be moved underground with the aid of the light crystals to make even the deepest tunnels livable for our species.

Sean, my family and I picked the area we wanted for our homes. They were near Yari's own quarters by his own requests. Sean also turned out to be surprisingly knowledgeable on how to bring fresh air into the tunnel systems and how to keep the crystals charged using electrical current. His experiments worked remarkably well. The biggest challenge he faced; was waking his people.

We knew they would be terribly upset, and that we had no way of returning them to their home world. While our battle to reclaim this world from the greed of the upper caste had not gone in a way we would have predicted: we had a great deal of challenges still ahead of us. I hoped that my mate's people would come to love their new world, but I had my doubts.

My belly was slowly swelling with the eggs that I would lay in a few more weeks' time. I was still not happy about being the one to become gravid. I hoped my mate did not want to have many offspring, I did not like this process. My mother kept telling me that I would get used to it, but at this point I was miserable and just wanted it to be over. My mate was trying to be supportive, but he didn't know any more about what was happening to me than I did. I had no interest in sex at all, and hadn't since I had conceived. My mother insisted that I would be back to normal once I laid but I was skeptical. I didn't think I would ever go back to normal after this.

CHAPTER THIRTEEN

Sean

I held De'Ceer as he shifted his body back and forth in discomfort. His mother rubbed his stomach with oils that she said would help speed the process. She had already had me insert a large amount of oil up inside of my mate. She said it would help the eggs to come down easier and with far less pain. For almost two days De'Ceer had fretted, pacing constantly, moving things around and snapping at me for every little thing. His mother just laughed and told me that it was a sure sign he would lay soon. I kept envisioning a lizard laying a cluster of leathery eggs.

De'Ceer snarled at me that I was too hot.

I chuckled and moved away from him, I knew he would snarl at me a few minutes later that he was too cold and wanted me to hold him again. We had been doing this for hours. I was trying not to snicker at him because I knew he was really uncomfortable.

His mother checked him again and gave a nod, "It won't be long now. He is opening." She continued to massage at his stomach and he grunted and I watched his stomach muscles ripple under his smooth scales. He arched his body and let out a pained growl.

"Sean, you need to help him. He is too tense. If he tightens up like that again and doesn't let the eggs drop, he will cause himself much pain and this will take far longer than it should. It also puts your offspring at risk. My son, you need to turn over and crouch now. You are too tense." His mother guided him to the right position and I wrapped my arms around his chest, under his arms. He panted, and I heard him say he hated me more than once.

"Forgive him for what he says right now, he will feel guilty about it later." His mother chuckled.

"It's the same with human woman." I ran my hand down his back, and he arched his chest up and gasped.

"Oh... Oh!" His mother gasped and her head shot up. "Sean, you did say that your kind give live birth did you not?"

"Yes, we don't lay eggs."

"Then, I think you need to do this! I have no idea how

to deliver this offspring!" I could hear the near panic in her voice. Shit! Like I know a damned thing about delivering a baby! I traded places with her and looked down, sure enough, under De'Ceer's arched tail was a crowning head with dark hair. Oh my God. I rubbed some of the oil that his mother had been using on my hands and helped guide the baby's head out. With a few more pushes, the baby slid free. I turned it carefully over and patted its back and in moments it was crying. I turned the baby back over and looked it... him.. over. Oh my! He was such a blend of both our features. His mother fetched me towels and string along with a knife so I could cut the umbilical cord. I wrapped the still slimy baby in the towel and handed him to his grandmother. She seemed astonished.

"He is so different! Look at his skin, it's so smooth! His hands are like yours, but he has short claws. He has a tail, but it doesn't have a ridge down its length!"

I felt De'Ceers stomach and I still felt something inside. A few exhausted pushes later, he had birthed a second baby, smaller and with features more like his own people except he lacked a tail and had hair more like my own. I helped him pass the after birth, which his father took away to dispose of. De'Ceer lay slumped in our nest, holding our little boys when his father returned with guests.

Yari, Ruik and De'Ceer's brothers all clustered in the doorway, eager to see the babies that were not born in eggs as is typical of their people. As they were holding the babies, Yari commented on how warm the babies seemed to be. While human infants cannot regulate their own body temperatures very well, they are still warm blooded. It seemed that both of our little ones were warm blooded like me. That could prove to be an advantage to them in the long run. We required more food and water, but we did not suffer from the cold the way they did.

I spent a few days bonding with my little boys before Yari approached me about waking my people from sleep. They were having problems keeping the equipment stable without experienced personnel to run it. My suggestion was to have an underground area ready for them. I remembered how horrible it was when I awoke, being freezing cold and terrified. I wanted it to be an easier and less stressful situation for them. I also wanted them to receive translation implants before they awoke. Yari agreed that we would need to have an area that was warm, secure, and quiet for them. He also agreed that we would wake them in small groups rather than in one large group. We decided to use part of the mine and fill it with heating crystals so it was warm and brightly lit, but to close sections with fencing so that people could not come charging out to attack anyone. It took almost a week to get the areas ready, but in that time we had to bring over two dozen people out of cold sleep because their chambers were failing. Most were brought to the planet before they woke. A few were already waking as they were brought in, but we did our best to get their implants in and to insure that I was near to help calm them.

Needless to say, they were extremely upset and stressed. They struggled to accept where they were. When they had calmed, I would take them to the surface so they could see where they were. I carefully introduced them to the people on this world. We all learned a lot from the first couple dozen people that had been woken. They helped when it was time to wake the others. In all, there were almost eleven hundred humans who now needed to adjust to a very different way of life on a different world.

I was helping with the last group of people when I saw someone I knew. Dave lay on his side on the warming stone. I began to look around and found Manik and across the room was Scott. I also recognized quite a few others from the party. It would seem that it would not have mattered if I had gone to the part or not. They were shocked when they saw me, especially now that I had the scars on my face and chest. I introduced them to De'Ceer and to my sons. They were more than a little overwhelmed, but I thought that they would adapt faster than the others because they already trusted me.

The majority of the people that had been taken were from the same area I had been taken from. They essentially had taken anyone that they could grab during that night. People outside having an after party were easily taken. I should have thought of that before. I knew that there were other humans out there that had been sent to other places, but for now, we could not do anything for them. For now, I had my hands full with my little ones, my mate, and my friends as we settled into our new lives on Red World.

* * *

Author's Note

This is the first book of the Red World series and others will follow in time. I started writing this book a few years ago, then my life was taken over by my own little one. I hope to get more books in this series written soon!

AUTHOR BIO

I'm a 30 something stay at home mom of a very active little boy, a 3 legged rescued Indian street dog and a half Saint Bernard mix. My husband and I own a small farm in the Cascade Mountains of Washington State. I fell in love with reading as a child, and that love blossomed as I got older until I had turned into a positively voracious reader. My love of writing also started when I was very young. I finished my first short story more than 20 years ago, but I was afraid to publish due to being dyslexic. It took me 20 years to get up the courage to finally give it a shot, and now I'm very glad that I did.

30825918R00103

Printed in Poland
by Amazon Fulfillment
Poland Sp. z o.o., Wrocław